Claire LaZebnik

epic fail

HARPER TEEN

An Imprint of HarperCollinsPublishers

Library of Congress Cataloging-in-Publication Data
LaZebnik, Claire Scovell.
  Epic fail / Claire LaZebnik.—1st ed.
      p.   cm.
  Summary: In this modern take on *Pride and Prejudice*,
Elise Benton, who has just moved to California, is a junior
at an exclusive prep school where, in spite of her initial bad
impression, she finds herself attracted to the moody and hand-
some son of Hollywood's most famous celebrity couple.
  ISBN 978-0-06-192126-1
  [1. Interpersonal relations—Fiction.   2. Dating (Social
customs)—Fiction.   3.   Sisters—Fiction.   4.   Preparatory
schools—Fiction.   5. Schools—Fiction.   6. Social classes—
Fiction.   7. Los Angeles (Calif.)—Fiction.]   I. Title.
PZ7.L4496Ep 2011   2010040300
  [Fic]—dc22   CIP
                                                      AC

11 12 13 14 15   CG/BV   10 9 8 7 6 5 4 3
❖
First Edition

For Annie.
My little girl with the big brown eyes
is now tall and beautiful,
but she's still who she's always been,
and that's the kindest person I know.
And for all her friends,
each one more brilliant
and dedicated than the next.
The world will be a better place
once these girls are running it.

handed Juliana her shoes. "They're soaked."

"So are you," she pointed out.

"I know!" I said happily. I had forgotten how much fun it was to run through a sprinkler on a hot day. "I think I deserve a hug, don't you?" I advanced on her.

She screamed and shrank back. "Don't touch me!"

"You really think it's so great to be dry? It takes talent to get wet on a sunny day, you know. I'm a maverick. You guys are just sheep."

"*Baa*," Chase agreed.

"How about you?" I wheeled on Derek, who was watching us with that faint smile on his face.

He held his ground. "Do your worst, wet girl."

I stopped—I wasn't about to hug the guy for real—and threw up my arms in mock despair.

"Hold on." He leaned forward and flicked at something on my cheek, his eyes briefly meeting mine. "Blade of grass."

"How'd it get all the way up there?" I asked lightly.

"Some mysteries aren't meant to be solved."

I grinned at him, then remembered I didn't trust him. Man, I hated not being able to figure someone out.

And from the slightly uncertain look he gave me as we all went to class, I suspected he felt the same way.

one

The front office wasn't as crazy as you'd expect on the first day of school, which seemed to confirm Coral Tree Prep's reputation as "a well-oiled machine."

That was a direct quote from the Private School Confidential website I had stumbled across when I first Googled Coral Tree—right after my parents told me and my three sisters we'd be transferring there in the fall. Since it was on the other side of the country from where we'd been living—from where I'd lived my entire life—I couldn't exactly check it myself, and I was desperate for more information.

A well-oiled machine didn't sound too bad. But I was less thrilled to read that Coral Tree was "basically a country club masquerading as a school." The same anonymous writer added, "I've yet to see a student drive a car onto campus that's not a Porsche or a BMW. And even an AP math student would lose count of the

Louboutins on the girls here." Yuck.

But while I was clicking around that site, I learned about another private school in L.A. that had a "condom tree"—kids allegedly tossed their used condoms up into its branches—so I guess my parents could have done worse than, you know, *Coral* Tree.

True to the school's reputation, the administrator in the office was brisk and efficient and had quickly printed up and handed me and Juliana each a class list and a map of the school.

"You okay?" I asked Juliana, as she stared at the map like it was written in some foreign language. She started and looked up at me, slightly panicked. Juliana's a year older than me, but she sometimes seems younger— mostly because she's the opposite of cynical and I'm the opposite of the opposite of cynical.

Because we're so close in age, people frequently ask if the two of us are twins. It's lucky for me we're not, because if we *were*, Juliana would be The Pretty One. She and I do look a lot alike, but there are infinitesimal differences—her eyes are just a touch wider apart, her hair a bit silkier, her lips fuller—and all these little changes add up to her being truly beautiful and my being reasonably cute. On a good day. When the light hits me right.

I put my head closer to hers and lowered my voice. "Did you *see* the girls in the hallway? How much makeup they're all wearing? And their hair is perfect, like they spent hours on it. How is that possible?" Mine was in a ponytail. It wasn't even all that clean because our fourteen-year-old sister, Layla, had hogged the bathroom that morning and I'd barely had time to brush my teeth, let alone take a shower.

"It'll all be fine," Juliana said faintly.

"Yeah," I said, with no more conviction. "Anyway, I'd better run. My first class is on the other side of the building." I squinted at the map. "I think."

She squeezed my arm. "Good luck."

"Find me at lunch, okay? I'll be the one sitting by herself."

"You'll make friends, Elise," she said. "I know you will."

"Just *find* me." I took a deep breath and plunged out of the office and into the hallway—and instantly hit someone with the door. "Sorry!" I said, cringing.

The girl I'd hit turned, rubbing her hip. She wore an incredibly short miniskirt, tight black boots that came up almost to her knees, and a spaghetti-strap tank top. It was an outfit more suited for a nightclub than a day of classes, but I had to admit she had the right body for it. Her blond hair was beautifully cut, highlighted, and styled, and the makeup she wore really played up her pretty blue eyes and perfect little nose. Which was scrunched up now in disdain as she surveyed me and bleated out a loud and annoyed "FAIL!"

The girl standing with her said, "Oh my God, are you okay?" in pretty much the tone you'd use if someone you cared about had just been hit by a speeding pickup truck right in front of you.

It hadn't been *that* hard a bump, but I held my hands up apologetically. "Epic fail. I know. Sorry."

The girl I'd hit raised an eyebrow. "At least you're honest."

"At least," I agreed. "Hey, do you happen to know where room twenty-three is? I have English there in, like, two minutes and I don't know my way around. I'm new here."

The other girl said, "I'm in that class, too." Her hair was brown instead of blond and her eyes hazel instead of blue, but the two girls' long, choppy manes and skinny bodies had been cast from the same basic mold. She was wearing a narrow, silky turquoise tank top over snug boot-cut jeans and a bunch of multicolored bangles on her slender wrist. "You can follow me. See you later, Chels."

"Yeah—wait, hold on a sec." Chels—or whatever her name was—pulled her friend toward her and whispered something in her ear. Her friend's eyes darted toward me briefly, but long enough to make me glance down at my old straight-leg jeans and my THIS IS

WHAT A FEMINIST LOOKS LIKE T-shirt and feel like I shouldn't have worn either.

The two girls giggled and broke apart.

"I know, right?" the friend said. "See you," she said to Chels and immediately headed down the hallway, calling brusquely over her shoulder, "Hurry up. It's on the other side of the building and you *don't* want to be late for Ms. Phillips's class."

"She scary?" I asked, scuttling to keep up.

"She just gets off on handing out EMDs."

"EMDs?" I repeated.

"Early morning detentions. You have to come in at, like, seven in the morning and help clean up and stuff like that. Sucks. Most of the teachers here are pretty mellow if you're a couple of minutes late, but not Phillips. She's got major control issues."

"What's your name?" I asked, dodging a group of girls in cheerleader outfits.

"Gifford." *Really? Gifford?* "And that was Chelsea you hit with the door. You really should be more careful."

Too late for that advice—in my efforts to avoid bumping into a cheerleader, I had just whammed my shoulder on the edge of a locker. I yelped in pain. Gifford rolled her eyes and kept moving.

I caught up again. "I'm Elise," I said, even though

5

she hadn't asked. "You guys in eleventh grade, too?"

"Yeah. So you're new, huh? Where're you from?"

"Amherst, Mass."

She actually showed some interest. "That near Harvard?"

"No. But Amherst College is there. And UMass."

She dismissed that with an uninterested wave. "You get snow there?"

"It's Massachusetts," I said. "Of course we do. Did."

"So do you ski?"

"Not much." My parents didn't, and the one time they tried to take us it was so expensive that they never repeated the experiment.

"We go to Park City every Christmas break," Gifford said. "But this year my mother thought maybe we should try Vail. Or maybe Austria. Just for a change, you know?"

I didn't know. But I nodded like I did.

"You see the same people at Park City every year," she said. "I get sick of it. It's like Maui at Christmas, you know?"

I wished she'd stop saying "You know?"

Fortunately, we had reached room 23. "In here," said Gifford. She opened the door and went in, successfully communicating that her mentoring ended at the room's threshold.

* * *

Over the course of the next four hours, I discovered that:

1. Classes at Coral Tree Prep were really small. When we got to English, I was worried that half the class would get EMDs or whatever they were called because there were fewer than a dozen kids in the room. But when Ms. Phillips came in, she said, "Good—everyone's here, let's get started," and I realized that *was* the class.

2. The campus grounds were unbelievably green and seemed to stretch on for acres. I kept gazing out the window, wishing I could escape and go rolling down the grassy hills that lined the fields.

3. Teachers at Coral Tree Prep didn't like you to stare out the window and would tell you so in front of the entire class who would then all turn and stare at The New Girl Who Wasn't Paying Attention.

4. Everyone at Coral Tree Prep was good-looking. Really. Everyone. I didn't see a single fat or ugly kid all morning. Maybe they just locked them up at registration and didn't let them out again until graduation.

5. Girls here wore every kind of footwear imaginable, from flip-flops to spike-heeled mules to UGG boots (despite the sunny, 80-degree weather), EXCEPT for sneakers. I guess those marked you as fashion-impaired.

6. I was wearing sneakers.

two

There are all these clichés about what it's like to be the new kid at school, like in movies, when you see people playing pranks on them or ostracizing them or publicly ridiculing them. I had no previous experience at being new: I had gone to only one public elementary school, which fed into my middle school, which fed into my old high school. So I don't know what I had been expecting, but the reality was more boring than anything else.

People were all willing to acknowledge me, ask me if I was new and what my name was, welcome me to the school (literally, several kids said, "Welcome to Coral Tree!"), and then they lost interest and went back to talking to their friends. I was isolated but not ostracized, ignored but not abused.

Still, it was stressful sitting alone and trying to look like I was fascinated by the posters on the various classroom walls whenever the other kids were chatting, so I was *very* happy to spot Juliana waiting in the cafeteria line when lunch break finally rolled around.

"Hey, you!" I ran over and just barely restrained myself from hugging her.

"Hey, yourself," she said calmly.

"How's it going? No one's talking to me. Is anyone talking to you?"

"Actually," she said, "people have been really nice."

"That's great." I wanted to be happy for her, but I had been looking forward to sharing the misery. "So what are you going to eat?"

"I don't know." She gave a vague look around. "Salad maybe? I'm not that hungry."

"You're not? I'm starving." It wasn't until I had grabbed a huge turkey sub and Juliana was balancing a dainty little green salad on her tray that it occurred to me there was something weird about Juliana's not being hungry. Usually she had a pretty healthy appetite. The only other time I could remember her not wanting to eat (when she wasn't sick) was the year before, when she had a crush on a guy in her Health and Human Fitness class. That had not ended well—the guy turned out to be a total tool.

As I moved through the cafeteria line, I saw raw

tuna sushi. And pomegranate seeds. And tamales. And Nutrisystem shakes. And sausage sticks made out of ostrich meat.

We definitely weren't in Massachusetts anymore.

I passed by a guy grabbing a can of soda out of the cold case. He was at least six feet tall, broad-shouldered, dark-haired, and way cuter than any guy at my old school, which had been full of highly cerebral and physically underdeveloped faculty brats. (To give you an idea: we had both a varsity and junior varsity debate team, but only enough recruits for a single basketball team.) While Juliana and I waited in line to pay, I glanced over my shoulder at him again—I'm not usually a gawker, but I'd had a tough morning and deserved a little pleasure.

I balanced my tray against my hip, checked the line—still a few people ahead of us—and stole another glance at Handsome Guy.

Whose gorgeous eyes met mine as he turned around, soda in hand. He gave me a vaguely annoyed and weary look—a look that said, *I'm so done with people staring at me*—and turned on his heel. Guess I wasn't as subtle as I thought. Blushing furiously, I turned back to the cashier before I embarrassed myself any more.

After we'd paid, Juliana led the way out of the cafeteria to the picnic tables scattered around the school courtyard.

"Outside tables?" I said. "What do they do when it rains?"

"It's L.A.," Juliana said absently, turning her head from side to side like she was searching for something. "It doesn't rain."

"That's got to be an exaggeration. How about there?" I pointed to an empty table. I just wanted to be alone with Jules, have a few minutes to relax before starting all over again with the afternoon classes.

But she was on the move, marching deliberately toward one of the tables—

Where some guy was rising to his feet and exuberantly waving her over, then gesturing down at the empty space next to him, like he'd been expecting her.

And she was going right toward him.

Suddenly, her loss of appetite made sense.

His name was Chase Baldwin, and he was definitely, unmistakably cute: blue-eyed with wavy brown hair and a ready smile. He was wearing a plain white oxford unbuttoned over a T-shirt, but something about the way they fit made him look put together, like an Abercrombie model (well, like an Abercrombie model who had remembered to put on a shirt that morning).

Without meeting my eyes, Juliana introduced us, explained that they'd met in history class, and slid into the space next to him. I sat down across from them. The benches and the long wooden tables they lined were surprisingly smooth and unblemished—a little dirty and sun-faded, maybe, but nothing was rotted or chipped. Apparently, even furniture wasn't allowed to age in this appearance-obsessed town.

I studied the huge sandwich on my plate and realized I had forgotten to get any utensils or even a napkin. I knocked the bread off the top and tore off a little piece of turkey, which I rolled into a compact bite I could pop neatly into my mouth.

Of course Chase chose that exact moment to lean forward and ask me a question. "How's your first day going, Elise?"

I made a *Sorry, I'm chewing* face, and he waited patiently until I swallowed and said, "Fine. There's a lot to get used to, but everyone's been nice. It helps to know Jules is nearby."

"That's really cute that you call her Jules," he said and grinned at her. "I like your nickname."

She made a face. "It's silly, but Elise started calling me that like three years ago and it stuck."

"You have a nickname, too?" he asked me.

"I could tell you, but then I'd have to shoot you," I said apologetically.

He nudged Juliana's elbow with his. "Will *you* tell me?"

"No way. She knows where I sleep."

"I'll get it out of you later." He munched on a chip.

"So is it just me or was that a terrifying amount of work Rivera assigned in history for the first day? He's famously tough, you know."

"Tough but good?" Juliana asked hopefully. She hadn't even touched her salad, just taken a few sips of her Diet Coke.

"Tough but boring." Chase wiped his mouth with a napkin. "Although today I was too fascinated by his hairpiece to be bored."

"It's a toupee?" Juliana said. "Really?"

"You didn't notice? It's a completely different color from the hair on the sides. Check it out next time. A kid who graduated last year told me that it was all twisted around one day, but Rivera didn't notice and taught the whole class like that. You'll probably have him next year," he added, glancing over at me, like he wanted to make sure I felt included in the conversation. There was a warmth to his gaze that gave me the sense there was nowhere he'd rather be than right here, having this conversation. Then he glanced up, looking past my shoulder. "There you are!" he said to whoever was standing behind me. "What took you so long?"

"Had to run back to my locker for my lunch." The voice was deep. I swiveled to get a look and was both pleased and unnerved to see it was the tall guy I'd been ogling in the cafeteria.

"You're *bringing* lunch this year?" Chase said. "That's a new one."

A shrug. "My mom's on this raw food kick and wants me to do it too."

"Oh, man, that's rough."

"It's worse for her cook. Mind if I sit here?"

I realized he was talking to me, quickly shook my head, and moved over. I noticed as I slid my tray down that some of the kids at the far end of the table had turned to watch as Chase's friend sat down.

He swung his leg over the bench as he plunked a can of soda and a long stainless-steel cylinder on the table. He settled in next to me, and I had to shift over even more. This guy took up a lot of space.

So it was my lucky day, right? Handsome Guy was sitting two inches away from me. I stole a peek at him and noticed—now that he was up close—that his eyelashes were so thick and dark, he almost looked like he was wearing eyeliner. Girls would have killed for those lashes.

They didn't look so bad on him, either.

He pulled the tab on his soda. As he raised it to his lips, he caught me staring at him—for the second time that day. He sighed heavily and looked away.

Way to make a first impression, Elise. Oh, wait— second impression. Both bad.

"Is Coke part of the diet?" Chase asked jovially.

"It's not cooked, right?" He took a big gulp.

"Derek, meet Juliana and Elise." Chase gestured toward each of us in turn. "They're both new. And they're sisters—but you can kind of tell that, can't you? This is Derek," he informed us.

"Hi," Derek said, a little warily.

We nodded and smiled and said hi back. There was a pause, like he and Chase were waiting for us to say something else. When we didn't, Derek turned his attention to deconstructing the stainless-steel cylinder, which turned out to be a set of small matching containers that all screwed together, and which he now carefully laid out on the table in a row in front of him. He opened the first one and sniffed dubiously at the unidentifiable brownish contents.

"That looks disgusting," Chase said.

"I don't even know what it is."

"Dump it and get something else, man."

"I promised my mother I wouldn't."

"Did you also promise her you wouldn't grab a slice of pizza after school?"

Brief smile. "Not in so many words."

"Sounds like a plan."

"Derek!" a new voice exclaimed. "You're back! Oh my God, how was it?" There was an impatient tap on my shoulder. "Excuse me—do you mind?"

I looked up and recognized the pretty girl I had bumped into that morning. She was with her pal Gifford again.

She recognized me at the same moment. "Oh, it's you. Hi. Hit anyone with a door lately? JK. Can you move, though? I need to sit next to Derek—I haven't seen him all summer."

There was plenty of space on the other side of me, so I slid down obediently while Chase nodded a casual greeting in her direction and said all our names by way of introducing everyone.

As Chelsea took my old place, Gifford plopped her tray on the table between us and waited expectantly. I sighed and slid down some more so she could sit between me and "Chels," who had taken hold of Derek's arm.

"So how was it?" she asked him eagerly. "Fantastic? Was it fantastic? It was, wasn't it?"

"Did you see a kangaroo?" Gifford chimed in before he could respond. She unwrapped a container of sushi and pushed it toward Chelsea. "We're sharing, remember. And don't forget I paid this time so you have to next time."

Chelsea ignored her. "I am so jealous," she said to Derek. "We didn't go anywhere all summer long except Belize and Costa Rica. And to visit our grandparents in New York. Oh, and that endless cruise to Alaska. That was so cheesy, though, it doesn't count."

"Derek just got back from Australia," Chase explained to Juliana.

"Wow," she said. "That's so cool."

"The beaches were nice," Derek said with an indifferent shrug.

"Did you see a kangaroo?" Gifford asked again. She seemed a little obsessed with the kangaroo thing.

"Yeah, a couple. But not on the street or anything—just in animal parks."

"I am so jealous," Chelsea moaned.

"Eh, seen one kangaroo, seen 'em all." Derek tentatively poked his fork into another container—something green and slimy this time. "They look like overgrown rats."

"They can punch people, right?" Gifford said. "Aren't they basically, like, pro boxers."

"I think that's only in cartoons," Chase said, and he and Juliana exchanged a grin.

"Do you have pictures?" Chelsea asked Derek. "Can we see them?"

"Maybe later."

"I want to see them, too," Gifford said. "Can I see them, too?"

"What made you choose Australia?" Juliana asked Derek.

There was a slight pause, like she had said something

awkward, but I had no clue why. Was she supposed to know why the guy we'd never met before had just vacationed halfway across the world?

"Movie shoot," he finally muttered.

"Movie shoot?" she repeated blankly.

"He was keeping his mom company," Chase added, like *that* explained it.

"Oh." Jules shot me a questioning look, and I shrugged to indicate that I had no more idea than she did who Derek's mother was, and everyone else was acting like we should already know, which made it impossible to be normal and just *ask*.

Derek seemed to have caught our silent exchange. He was watching us curiously, like something about us was confusing to him.

"Oh God, *look* at her!" Chelsea exclaimed suddenly.

"Someone offend your fashion sense by wearing sandals with socks again, Chelsea?" Chase joked. "My sister takes these things very seriously," he told Juliana.

"I didn't realize she was your sister." Jules looked at me again, and I shook my head—I hadn't known that, either.

I felt like we needed SparkNotes for this whole lunch.

"No, seriously," Chelsea said. "It's *her*. The new principal. The one everyone hates already."

We all looked up at that and saw her, the new principal, charging around the picnic tables, stopping to pat one kid on the shoulder, exchange a word with another, admonish a third who had let a wrapper blow onto the ground without picking it up, and so on.

"She looks totally crazy," Chelsea said. "Which I hear she *is*. They say they only hired her because the guy they really wanted took another job at the last second so they were stuck and she was the only candidate who was still, you know, *available*, because no one else would take her."

The new principal did look a little nuts. She was wearing a reasonably businesslike dark red suit, but she had matched it with a bright chartreuse top with an enormous bow at the collar, navy tights, and brown pumps. Her graying brown hair had been pinned up in a bun at some earlier point in time, but it was the kind of kinky, wavy hair that plots its escape from the moment you try to capture it, and wisps were flying all over the place.

Her wire-rimmed glasses were slightly askew. My fingers itched with the urge to straighten them as she stopped at a table near us and asked the kids sitting there if they had any suggestions for improving the cafeteria.

"Serve Frappuccinos," said one girl.

"And Pinkberry!" said another.

"Free booze," shouted a boy at the far end of the table.

"Who said that?" asked the principal sharply, swiveling to look in the direction the voice had come from. A lot of boys were sitting there. They all grinned at her innocently. "That's not funny."

"Oh, for God's sake," Chelsea said. "The woman can't take a joke. Despite quite clearly *being* one." She picked up her empty cup and climbed over the bench. "Anyone else need something from the caf?"

I was about to ask her to grab me a fork and napkin when the principal turned and called out, "Excuse me. You there! What's your name?"

As Chelsea begrudgingly told her, Juliana and I sank down lower in our seats.

"Well, Chelsea, it's nice to meet you." The principal held out her hand, and Chelsea shook it, with her lip curling so high, I thought it was going to enter her right nostril. "I'm Dr. Gardiner."

"Yeah, I know."

Dr. Gardiner tilted her head sideways, which made her glasses look almost straight. "Let's talk about the dress code, Chelsea."

"You mean, like, uniforms?" Chelsea said. "We don't have uniforms here. Haven't you noticed?"

"But we do have a dress code." Dr. Gardiner gestured toward Chelsea's legs. "And I'm afraid that skirt doesn't conform to it."

Chelsea put her hands on her hips. "This is a Dolce and Gabbana, and our tailor *just* hemmed it."

"He hemmed it too much: skirts can't be more than four inches above the knee." The new principal reached into her pocket and pulled out a tape measure. "Let's check."

Chelsea took a step back. "No way."

Dr. Gardiner shrugged. "Fine, but I'm going to have to ask you to change."

"Change into *what*? It's not like I keep an extra wardrobe in my locker."

"You can wear your PE shorts."

"You have *got* to be kidding me! Do you know how dorky those are?"

The principal slipped the measuring tape back into her pocket. "If I see you still wearing that skirt later today, I'll have to notify your parents and send you home."

Chelsea's mouth opened so wide in horror that I could see the wisdom teeth budding in the back, but the principal's attention had moved on. "How is everyone enjoying his or her lunch?" she asked, gazing along our table. That's when she spotted Juliana. "Hello!" she said delightedly. "How's your first day going, sweetie?"

Juliana managed a weak smile. "Fine?" she said.

"Good, good. Oh, there you are, Elise! Everything going well?"

"Yeah, fine," I said. "Everything's fine." *Please go away*, I thought. *Please, please go away.*

Dr. Gardiner said, "Well, I'm happy to hear that." She turned. My stomach muscles relaxed: she was leaving. Wait, no—she was just picking up a protein bar wrapper that was lying on the ground. She carefully balled it up in her hand as she stood back up. Then she beamed at us like the proud mother she was and opened her mouth to effectively kill our short-lived anonymity. "Won't you girls introduce me to your new friends?"

"She's your *mother*?" Chelsea said a few minutes later, after Dr. Gardiner had finally moved on. "How can you stand going home at night?"

"Chels," said her brother warningly. "That's not—"

"Seriously," she said. "Is she always that bad? And why don't you guys give her some fashion tips?" Her eyes fell on my T-shirt. "Or not."

The insult hardly registered: I was still trying to process the shock of discovering that Chase's friend Derek was the son of Melinda Anton and Kyle Edwards, the most famous celebrity couple in the country, and the embarrassing realization that everyone at the table, including my mother, had already known this except me and Juliana.

Melinda was *the* leading female action star in the U.S. She'd starred in an endless series of blockbuster movies. Kyle was more of the indie film type, but he'd won an Oscar or two, so he was no slouch.

They were on the cover of half the tabloids on the newsstands any given week of the year.

But okay, fine—I guess if I'd thought about it, I'd have expected a private school in L.A. to boast a celebrity brat or two. No big deal, right?

Except that it seemed to be one for my mother—hence the awkwardness, above and beyond the fact that she was our principal, which would have been bad enough. For someone who always maintained that movies were a waste of time and money, she got awfully excited when she realized who Derek was: she kept telling him over and over again how "empowering" his mother's movies were to young girls and how his father was "not just an actor—he's an *artist*." The true horror came when she informed Derek that I—her second oldest daughter—was also very creative and liked to make my own "little movies." (I had taken one stupid summer class in filmmaking two years ago.)

Derek nodded briefly as she chattered away, but showed no interest in discussing his parents, just chewed steadily and unenthusiastically on the little brown bits of earth or whatever it was in his lunch rocket. Eventually, my mother ran out of things to say and left with a satisfied wave.

But she'd stayed long enough, judging by the expressions on the faces around us. Chase looked sympathetic, Chelsea looked horrified, and Derek looked like he smelled something bad—although, admittedly, that could have just been his revolting lunch. Gifford, at least, looked indifferent.

"Go change your skirt, Chelsea," Chase said. "Mom will flip if you get a suspension."

"I'm going to call Linda"—she pronounced the name with a Spanish accent, *Leenda*—"and tell her to bring me something decent to wear. No way am I wearing those disgusting PE shorts in public."

"You'd better hurry," Chase said. "Lunch will be over in ten minutes."

"I have a free period next." She pulled a bejeweled iPhone out of her Prada bag and started punching furiously at it before putting it to her ear. Pretty soon she was chattering away fluently in pissy Spanish.

"Wow," Chase said after an awkward moment of silence. "I had no idea Dr. Gardiner was your mom. But your last name—?"

"—is Benton," Juliana said with a slightly nervous laugh. "She kept her maiden name."

"Wait," he said. "Isn't there a new math teacher

named Benton? Don't tell me that's your father."

"Sort of."

He pursed his lips in a silent whistle.

"For what it's worth, I'm pretty sure we're not related to any of the lunch ladies," I said.

"Too bad." Chase turned to me with his ready smile. "I could use an in at the cafeteria."

"The sandwich lady does owe me a huge favor."

That actually caught Derek's interest. He looked up. "Really?"

"Oh, yeah," I said. "But it's a long story—involves this knife fight in Brussels back during the war. She was smuggling, I was a double agent for the resistance. . . . The usual."

"Is she always this nuts?" Chase asked Juliana.

"Pretty much."

"I'm hurt you don't believe me," I said.

"Get her to stop putting mayonnaise on my sandwich when I ask for 'no mayo,' and I'll believe you," Chase said.

"For God's sake, man, I'm not a miracle worker!"

"Just to be clear," Derek said, "this war you're talking about—" But he was interrupted by Chelsea, who suddenly interposed her body between us to poke at Gifford's empty sushi container. "Did you eat it *all*? I thought we were sharing."

"I totally offered you some." Gifford stood up. "Jesus,

Chels, don't keep changing your mind and blaming me."
She stepped over the bench.

"Whatever. I'll tell Linda to pick me up a sandwich since she's coming anyway." She took out her phone again. "Oh, that reminds me—I need a ride home today, Chase."

"You mind going out for pizza with me and Derek first?"

"Are you kidding?" she said. "That's even better. I'll just wait to eat until then."

"Can I come, too?" Gifford asked eagerly.

Chelsea twisted her mouth. "Oh God, Gifford, I don't think that'll work. Sorry, but I have a *lot* of homework. Let's do it another time." She touched Derek's shoulder. "So I'll see you after school? I am *so* glad you're back." Her hand lingered on his arm as she smiled prettily down at him, letting her pretty hair bounce prettily along her pretty collarbone and pretty shoulders.

Man, I thought. *She really likes him.* I'd always wondered what it would be like to have an older brother who could bring friends home for me to date—guess it would be like this.

Did Derek like her as much as she liked him? Hard to tell. All he said now was, "See you," and since he didn't even really look up, he totally missed all that prettiness on display for him.

Chelsea and Gifford said a general good-bye and

moved across the courtyard together.

I shifted over a little, just to fill in some of the space on the bench. Chase and Juliana were talking quietly, which left me and Derek sitting there in silence.

I was still trying to process the fact that the guy sitting two feet away from me had parents who were world-famous. We didn't have movie stars in Amherst.

I studied the table in front of me, running my fingers over the unblemished surface. It wasn't wood at all, I realized. It was plastic made to look like wood. No wonder it wasn't splintering or rotting.

The silence was getting more awkward. I felt like one of us should say something. So I tried. "How's the raw food thing going?"

"Sucks," was the helpful response.

"What's the theory with that diet anyway? Is it supposed to be better for you because it's not cooked? Nutrients more nutritious? Vitamins more . . . vitamitious?"

That elicited a very small smile. "Something like that, I guess."

Five more words: I was making progress. Next topic. "So what was the movie your mom was making in Australia? Will it be out soon?"

The edges of his mouth tightened. "I don't know." He threw down his fork and started to close the containers. "I give up," he said to Chase. "I can't eat any more of this crap. If I don't see you later, I'll meet you at Romano's." He quickly packed up the steel cylinder while I sat there feeling totally brushed off and annoyed about it: I was just trying to make polite conversation. If he didn't like my choice of topic, he could have come up with one of his own.

"Hey, you want to come with us?" Chase asked Juliana. "Get some pizza after school? You too, Elise."

"We can't," Jules said. "We have to drive our little sisters home."

"Bring them along."

Derek froze halfway to his feet and stared at Chase. He didn't wave his arms and scream, *No! For the love of God, no!* but the look on his face pretty much got that message across.

I quickly said, "I can drive the girls home, Jules. And that way you could—"

"No, no, I think you should all come," Chase insisted. "Your sisters will love it—how old are they, anyway?"

"Layla's fourteen," Juliana said. "Kaitlyn's ten. But—"

"Great." Chase rose to his feet. "Romano's is on the southwest corner of San Vicente and Montana. But maybe I'll see you before then. What classes do you have after lunch?"

Juliana thought a moment. "Uh . . . math. And then

English. And then Visual Arts One."

"Who for English?"

"Feinberg."

"Me too!" His delight seemed genuine. "Save me a seat if you get there first." He swung his leg over the bench. "Bye, Elise. Nice to meet you."

"Same here."

"Later," said Derek Edwards without looking at either me or Jules. He grabbed his lunch silo and left the table without another word. Chase followed after him with one last cheery wave.

"Are we really going to go out for pizza with them?" I asked Jules as we picked up our trays and carried them to the trash cans.

"I'm not sure we should." Her brow was creasing the way it did when she was uneasy. She added her tray to the stack on top of the trash can. "He probably felt like he had to invite us since we were sitting right there."

I emptied my tray in the trash and put it on top of hers. "I think he really wanted *you* to go. But he probably was just being polite about the rest of us."

"I don't want to go alone. So either we all go or none of us."

"Derek looked kind of annoyed when Chase said to bring everyone."

"I think that's just the way he always looks." Jules

grinned wickedly at me. "But we shouldn't judge—maybe the poor guy has a rash in an awkward place."

I laughed. "That *would* explain why he's so irritable." We started walking back toward the building. "Especially about his parents—he acted like no one had the right to talk about them."

"Yeah, I noticed that, too." A beat. "Chase is nice, though, isn't he?"

I nodded and sneaked a glance at her face. Yep. All starry-eyed and hopeful and excited, just like she sounded.

I watched her head off toward her next class with a slightly anxious feeling in my throat. Chase did seem nice. But this school—this city—was like nothing we'd known before, and I had a feeling that someone like Juliana could get chewed up and spat out in a second.

I'd just have to look out for her, that was all. I always had and I always would.

three

Gifford turned out to be in my Honors French class. To my surprise she actually came over and swung her slender body into the chair next to mine.

"Can you believe Chelsea?" she said by way of a greeting. "I mean, that whole Romano's thing? Like she has time to have pizza if I'm not there, but not if I am?" She leaned her head close to mine and lowered her voice. "I know why. She totally has a crush on Derek and doesn't want any competition." She rolled her eyes. "But hello-o! Everyone knows he only hangs out with her because he's been friends with her brother since, like, preschool. It has nothing to do with *her*." She snaked her phone out of her purse and, hiding it on her lap below the desk, stole a glance at it. "I texted her about it, but she's deliberately ignoring me. I *know* she keeps her phone on vibrate during class."

"You can come with us, if you want," I said.

"To Romano's? What do you mean? Did Chelsea invite you?"

"Chase did."

"Why?" Maybe not the most tactful question, but it was clear she was just surprised, not trying to be rude.

"I don't know. He was being nice, I guess. We have room in the car if you want to come."

"God, Chelsea will be so pissed if I just show up!" She seemed delighted at the thought. "I can't wait to see the expression on her face! Let me just text my mom." She tapped quickly before putting the phone away because class was starting, but when she checked at the end of the hour, her mother had reminded her that the tennis coach was coming that afternoon. ("Coming"— that meant she took lessons at her house. That meant she had a tennis court in her backyard. My family barely had a backyard in our backyard.) As we picked up our books, a disappointed Gifford informed me that the coach charged if you canceled less than twenty-four hours in advance so she couldn't go to Romano's, but my invitation had clearly won me some points. She even said we should "hang" that weekend. So I guess I'd made a friend. A kind of annoying one, admittedly, but better than nothing.

After French, I had astronomy, my elective for the semester. I realized the class wasn't limited to juniors when I spotted Derek Edwards sitting in the first row, his long, muscular arms and legs dangling from every side of the too-small desk/chair combo he was sitting in. He was paging through a book.

I moved to the back of the room and took a seat close to the wall where I could watch the floor show: girls hurling themselves into the desks around Derek. I should have guessed that his combination of good looks and Hollywood status would be catnip to the school's female population. That explained his weary resignation when he'd caught me staring at him in the cafeteria.

The girls surrounded him, tossing their books onto the desks to mark their territory before stripping off their sweaters to show off the tiny, close-fitting tank tops and camisoles they wore underneath. They slid into seats, crossing legs that were either bare from the bottoms of their short skirts to the tops of their tall boots or else outlined and cupped by tight stretch jeans.

A lot of the boys seemed equally eager to get Derek's attention, calling out to him as they passed, one of them inviting him to a party that weekend, which apparently was going to be "mind-blowingly awesome!"

I don't know why they were all so into him: he barely responded, just read his book with an occasional glance up, slouching so far down in his seat that his long legs stuck out in the aisle where they tripped a lanky guy who saved himself from falling only by grabbing the edge of a desk.

Derek didn't apologize. He looked up, scowled like *he* had been injured in some way, and went back to reading.

The guy who'd stumbled didn't seem at all fazed, just continued on to my part of the room. "Mind if I sit here?" His hair was a wavy chestnut color and his eyes were a grayish blue that caught the light as he gestured to the seat on my right.

"It's all yours," I said with a smile.

He collapsed into the seat, dropping his book bag onto the desktop with a groan. "Heavy," he announced. Then he curled his body toward me. "You new here? Or am I falling victim once again to my bad facial recognition skills and you're going to tell me we've been in school together since kindergarten?"

"I'm hurt you don't remember me," I said. "What with my being your cousin and all."

He hit his forehead with the palm of his hand. "Of course! Mother's side or father's?"

"Both."

"See, that's the problem," he said. "You look like a mixture. Made it hard to recognize you." He held out his hand. "Webster Grant." We shook.

Chelsea Baldwin entered the classroom. Her face lit

up when she saw Derek, but there were no empty chairs left near him.

"That's a great name," I said to Webster Grant.

"Sure, if you like being named after a dictionary and a president. But it could have been worse—at least I'm not Random House Obama." I laughed and he nodded approvingly. "She has a sense of humor. So what's your name?"

"Elise Benton."

"I have no jokes for that one. Not yet anyway." He studied me thoughtfully. "You're not *really* my cousin, right?"

"Well, if you go back far enough . . ."

"Like Adam and Eve back? Let's not. I don't actually like most of my cousins. But you—you have potential."

"Thank you," I said, feeling oddly pleased by the meaningless compliment.

A voice said, "Psst," and I twisted to my left. Chelsea was settling into the desk on that side, now wearing a pair of tight jeans and an even tighter tissue-thin cashmere sweater. My mother hadn't said she needed to change her top, so I assumed Chelsea just wasn't happy unless she was wearing a complete outfit. Which also explained the unnecessary change from boots to pink spike-heeled shoes.

All right, to be honest, I kind of lusted after the shoes. Mom would never let me wear anything that high or that dressy to school, and they were really cute.

"What?" I asked. Chelsea crooked her finger and beckoned me closer. I leaned toward her with diminishing patience and repeated, "What?"

She folded her hands primly on the desk in front of her. "Even though your mother totally ruined my day, I'm going to be nice and give you some good advice because you shouldn't punish people for what their parents do." She jerked her chin in Webster's direction and lowered her voice. "Don't get too friendly with him."

I blinked. "Excuse me?"

"He's a total loser," she said. "No one likes him. And if you start hanging out with him, you'll be buying yourself a one-way ticket to Loserville City."

"Is that anywhere near Dorktown Village?" I clasped my hands with mock excitement. "I was hoping to see that just once before I die."

Her nostrils flared. "I'm just trying to help."

"And I'm just trying to appreciate it."

Webster was now reclining comfortably in his seat, his long legs crossed in front of him, his arms resting across the desk, the picture of laziness. He winked at me. "Princess Chelsea in a royal snit about something?" he asked with more amusement than annoyance.

I grinned, but before I could respond, the teacher strode into the room, calling for us all to "listen up."

Cantori was one of those youngish teachers who like to dress conservatively—today he wore a fitted sports coat and a narrow tie—and then prove they're still cool by spending class time slouching against the furniture and chatting with the kids instead of actually teaching them. These are the same ones who, after months of wasting time, suddenly realize report cards are coming due, at which point they'll mercilessly cram a semester's worth of homework and tests into a few days and destroy everyone's life for that week. I'd had teachers like him before and they weren't the worst, but they weren't the best, either.

His one concession to actually teaching astronomy that first day was to show us how to map the sky using Google Earth on the classroom's SMART Board.

When he got tired of that, he turned the lights back on and faced us. "Okay, class. So all year long we'll be talking about the stars. I'll be teaching you what they're made of, what we know about them, what we *don't* know about them—but before all that knowledge stuff begins, let's get a little silly and romantic here and talk about stars metaphorically. What's the first thing you think of when someone says the word *star*? It's a very evocative word. So I want to know what it means to each of you, personally." He looked around the silent classroom. "Chirp, chirp," he said.

"Fine. I'll start. 'Star light, star bright, first star I see tonight, I wish I may, I wish I might, have the wish I wish tonight.'" He paused. Silence. "Stars and wishing—always entwined, right?" More silence. "Who's next?" No one raised a hand. He pointed to a cute, compact, and curvy girl up near the front—one of Derek's fans. "Sylvie, you."

"Um," she said. She flipped her hair over her shoulder flirtatiously. "'Stars and Stripes Forever'?"

"A patriot! Excellent. Now someone else."

A girl called out, "The Star of David."

"No religion in the classroom!" Cantori barked. Then he waved his hand. "Nah, I'm just kidding. Okay, someone else?" He pointed to the raised hand next to me. "You?"

Chelsea purred, "Movie stars, of *course*." Her eyes settled on Derek's back as she spoke, but if the back had any interest in what she was saying, it didn't reveal it.

"Spoken like a true Angeleno," Cantori said. "Next!"

"Starbursts," a boy called out, and a girl said, "Yum!" and Sylvie added, "But not the tropical flavor ones—those are gross," and everyone laughed.

"Good, good, keep it going." Cantori's eyes fell on me. "You got one?"

"I know a quote about stars," I said.

"Let's hear it."

"'We are all in the gutter, but some of us are looking at the stars.'"

"One of my favorites." Cantori peered at me. "What's your name?"

"Elise."

"Good job, Elise." He looked around the classroom. "Anyone know who said that?"

"She did," said the boy who had said the Starbursts thing and was clearly gunning for the title of class comic.

Cantori heaved an exaggerated sigh. "Yes, Billy, but someone else said it first—"

"Oscar Wilde," said Derek Edwards abruptly.

"Score one for the big guy!" said Cantori. "You kids are impressing me more and more. Care to tell us what Wilde meant by that, Derek?"

I couldn't see Derek's face, but his shoulders twitched slightly in what looked from the back like an irritated shrug. "Basically it means the world's a giant shithole, but some of us are capable of imagining something better."

A lot of kids laughed. I wondered if Derek would get in trouble for swearing—no one at my old school would have dared say "shit" in front of a teacher. You could get suspended for that.

But Cantori beamed delightedly. "Exactly right, Derek." So this school was more easygoing than my

40

old one—or maybe it was if your mother was Melinda Anton.

Webster tilted sideways toward me. "Don't be too impressed," he whispered. "You know why Derek knows that?"

"Why?"

"Because his dad played Oscar Wilde in a movie. Bet you that line was right out of the screenplay."

"Oh." I felt slightly disappointed for a reason I couldn't quite pinpoint. I slid down in my chair as a kid near the window called out to Cantori, "StarKist tuna!"

Sylvie, the girl who had said the "Stars and Stripes" thing, lingered by Derek's side after the bell rang. As I passed them on my way toward the door, I heard her say, "So how many classes do we have together? There's this one and English, right?"

"That makes two," he said shortly. Then: "Hold on." I felt a tap on my arm and realized with surprise that the request was directed at me, not her.

I stopped and said, "Hi."

Sylvie said, "See you later, Derek?" He grunted non-committally and she flounced off.

"You guys coming to get pizza with us?" he asked me.

"Yeah. Is that okay?"

"Why wouldn't it be?" he said, like I was insane to think he'd ever been anything but warm and welcoming.

"I don't know." An awkward pause. "You knew the Oscar Wilde quote," I said.

"You like Wilde?"

"Sure. He was tortured, brilliant, funny, gay . . . basically my dream guy."

"Even the gay part?" he said with the ghost of a smile—which for all I knew was what passed for hysterical mirth with this guy.

"*Especially* the gay part," I said. "I'm weird that way."

"How's that working out for you?"

"I'm beginning to think it's not a good long-term romantic strategy." I shifted my messenger bag so the weight fell more comfortably over my shoulders. "Seriously, he's an amazing writer. I had to read *The Importance of Being Earnest* for English last year, and then I just kept reading everything he wrote. He's funny and sad at the same time."

He leaned his hip against one of the desks, relaxing into it like he was in no hurry to move along. "Funny and sad. That's exactly it."

"Webster said your dad played him in a movie?"

His face tightened in a way that made me sorry I'd brought up his father.

On the other hand . . . was it really so awful to mention his parents?

"Yeah, a long time ago." He glanced at his watch.

You know, it was lucky for him he was so good-looking. Made you want to connect with him despite his lack of response. So I worked to keep the conversation going, steering us back to Wilde. "They did *Earnest* at my old school a few years ago, and people were actually laughing like they were at a Will Ferrell movie or something. It was pretty—"

"Oh, good, you waited!" Webster suddenly materialized at my side. "Sorry I took so long—shoelace cooperation issues. Let me take you to your next class. Don't want our new girl to get lost," he said to Derek. He extended his fist for a bump. "How're you doing, big D? How's the family?"

Derek stared at Webster's outstretched hand for a second, breathed in sharply, then, without saying a word, pushed forward right past us, with a brief cold nod in my direction. It almost looked like he miscalculated the space because he knocked his shoulder hard against Webster's—*almost* looked like that, like it was an accident, but it wasn't. I could tell he had done it deliberately, had angled his shoulder forward so the hardest, sharpest part knocked Webster right into the desk behind him. Then he just kept going out the door.

I stared after him for a stunned moment, then spun around on my heel to check on Webster. "You okay?"

He rubbed his shoulder ruefully. "I'll live."

"What was that about? He and I were just standing there talking and then"—I tossed my hands in the
air—"boom."

"Crazy, right?" He gestured toward the door and
said, "Let's get out of here." In the hallway, I spotted
Derek's broad shoulders disappearing around a bend in
the corridor. Webster said in a low voice, "He can act
like a real jerk. But it's not his fault."

"Not his fault?" I repeated. "How can you be an
accidental jerk?"

Webster grinned down at me. His thin face lit up
when he smiled like that. He had dimples, not in the
center of his cheeks like a little girl, but narrow dents
up high. "Well, maybe it's a *little* his fault, but I actually feel sorry for him. Think about what it must be
like: your parents are so crazy-famous that everywhere
you go people are falling all over you, treating you like
you're something special, giving you stuff, trying to get
your attention. . . ." He gestured with his hands as we
walked. "You probably start thinking you're different
from everyone else—more important—but at the same
time you don't know whether people really like you for
yourself or just for the fact your parents are famous, so
you also get all insecure and paranoid. It probably plays
some intense games with your mind."

That fit exactly with what I'd seen. "But that doesn't
explain why he hit you."

He glanced around. "That's a longer story. Do you have a class now?"

"Yeah." I consulted my schedule and read, "Honors History. Kashani. Room nineteen."

"Kashani? Bring a magazine—you'll be bored. This way." We moved down the hallway, weaving through the crowds of kids talking and laughing. With Webster at my side, I didn't feel as much like a lonely outsider.

"So, does Derek have some kind of problem with you?" I asked.

"We actually used to be pretty good friends, and then . . . I don't know. He's what you might call mercurial."

"I might—if I liked to throw around SAT words."

He laughed. "How about 'moody' then?" he suggested. "Better?"

I nodded just as a girl in front of us bent down to tie her shoelace. We had to separate to go around her, then rejoined on the other side.

"There's got to be more to this story," I said.

"Smart girl. I'll tell you the whole saga when we've got more time. And I promise to stick to words of two syllables." He stopped in front of a door. "You said nineteen, right?"

"Uh-huh." But I didn't go in right away. "Hey, do you know Chase Baldwin at all?"

"Of course. Princess Chelsea's big brother."

"What about him? What's he like?"

"He's great. Everyone likes Chase. Proof? Even Derek likes him." A pause. "The bell's ringing," Webster pointed out.

"Sorry!" I said with a guilty start. "You're going to be late for your class."

"Well worth it," he said gallantly. "I'd risk a hundred tardies for the chance to chat with you again." He shifted his bag, held out his hand. We shook. "Good-bye, Elise. It was nice meeting you."

"Same here," I said, and walked into the classroom with a smile on my face.

four

was supposed to meet Juliana and Layla by the steps leading up to the parking lot as soon as school let out. I got there first and climbed partway up the stairs so I could watch everyone moving below me. I felt like a general wearily surveying the terrain of his next battle, except that I had no hope of actually winning the war that was high school.

Within a minute or two, I spotted Juliana walking slowly toward me, Chase Baldwin at her side, the two of them talking away earnestly. They looked like they'd known each other forever.

We'd both had our crushes and flirtations over the years, but we'd always spent more time talking to each other *about* the guys than actually talking *to* them. Our clumsy attempts at romance had ended in some extra sisterly bonding—and no actual relationships.

But this already felt different.

Juliana's eyes were cast down so I don't think she could see the way Chase was looking at her, but I could. He looked content, settled, like he belonged in the airspace next to this girl he'd met only a few hours earlier.

She looked up, saw me, and waved. They stopped walking then, but kept talking for a few more minutes while I waited and watched, waited and watched. I felt almost jealous of Jules—not because she'd found Chase, but because here, in this new setting, where I was just trying to get my bearings and survive, she was already thriving.

We'd always been inseparable, always been the two closest Benton sisters—buy one, get one free—and now, in addition to all the other changes of the last few months, it looked like that was going to change, too.

Finally, she broke away and came toward me.

"Hi," she said, a little too casually, as she joined me on the steps.

"You're going to be seeing him again in half an hour, you know. No need for a long good-bye."

She ignored that. "Where's Layla? She's late."

"Layla's always late."

"Not *always*."

"Always," I repeated.

Another fifteen minutes went by before Layla finally showed.

"You were supposed to meet us here at three thirty," I snapped.

"It's right around then, isn't it?" She glanced vaguely at her watch.

"It's almost four," Juliana said.

"Sorry. I met some girls today and we were talking and I didn't realize how late it had gotten."

"Why are your eyes all glittery?" I asked.

Layla reached up to touch her eyelid absently. "We were playing around with each other's makeup."

"You'd better take it off before Mom sees you," Juliana warned. We could get away with wearing a small amount of artfully applied blush and eye shadow so long as it looked fairly natural, but anything too bright was a red flag to our parents, who didn't think their daughters should wear makeup at all.

"I know," Layla said. "There are wipes in the car." She pushed me away from her. "Are you sniffing me, Elise? What are you, a dog?"

"Have you been *smoking*?" I asked.

"Oh, for God's sake! Can we just go home, please?" She ran up the rest of the steps.

Incredulous, I grabbed my messenger bag and

dashed after her, Juliana close behind. "If Mom and Dad find out—"

"They won't if you don't tell on me," she said over her shoulder. "Anyway, it wasn't me who was smoking. It was a couple of the other girls—their smoke got in my clothes. You can smell my breath, if you don't believe me."

"You're chewing gum! That's the oldest trick in the book."

"Yeah?" she said. "And how would *you* know that?"

"Give her a break, Elise." Juliana caught at my arm. "If she says she wasn't smoking, she wasn't smoking."

"Thank you," Layla said. "At least *someone* in this family is capable of showing some trust." She walked on the path ahead of us, her chin high, the picture of affronted dignity.

That was when I noticed her pockets. "No way!" I said to Juliana.

"What?"

I pointed. "Those are my jeans—the *one* new pair I own."

"Are you sure? Maybe they just look like yours."

"I'm sure," I said, my voice tight with the kind of frustration that comes from having three sisters and a small house and never getting to keep anything to yourself. "I bought them with my own money." I sped up. "I should tear them right off her little selfish—"

Juliana tightened her grip on my arm. "Calm down, Elise. She shouldn't have borrowed them without asking, but I know she was really nervous this morning. She was probably worried about being dressed right, and—"

I flung off her hand irritably. "Why do you always defend her?"

"Honestly?" She smiled apologetically. "Because someone has to."

We entered the student parking lot and walked by rows of Audis, Lexuses (Lexi?), Mercedes, and Porsches before going through the gate that separated the students' cars from the faculty's. The cars instantly became less fancy and more utilitarian.

Ours stood out among the countless gray-toned and indistinguishable small Japanese cars; it was one of only a few minivans, and uniquely bright green. Mom had negotiated for it years ago through a car dealer who said he could get us a great price as long as we weren't picky about the color.

We weren't picky about the color. We couldn't afford to be.

Layla was already tugging impatiently on the door handle. "Will you hurry up and open it already? My bag weighs a ton."

Juliana pulled out the keys and unlocked the van. We had driven in with Mom that morning, but she had told Juliana to take us home. Dad's old Honda was still in his space: he'd head home when he was ready and then come back to pick up Mom whenever she was all done with meetings—which, she had pronounced, wouldn't be until after dinner. She had a lot to do "to whip this school into shape," she had said in the car that morning, her eyes gleaming with almost-religious fervor.

As Layla tossed her book bag inside the car, I came up behind her. "If you ever wear my jeans again without permission, I'll kill you," I said.

She glanced down at her legs like she had never seen them before in her life. "Are these yours? I had no idea. They were in my room, so I just assumed they were mine."

"You are such a liar," I said. "They were folded and in my drawer this morning."

"You're obviously confused." It was the little snarky smile on her face that drove me to the edge. I grabbed her arm—not gently.

"I am so sick of this," I said, shaking her. "Why do you have to be such a—" Something fell out of the pocket of her hoodie. We both bent down to grab it, but I was faster. I snatched it up and showed the open cigarette pack to Juliana. "Still think she was telling the truth?"

"Oh, Layla," Juliana moaned.

"They're not mine," Layla said, turning to her. "I'm holding them for a friend." Her voice got higher. "Really. I swear."

"Do you ever stop lying?" I thrust the pack out toward her. "They were on your—"

A BMW convertible came roaring up to us too fast and then paused—just for a second, like the driver had tapped his brake.

And that was when I caught a glimpse of Derek Edwards's face through the driver's side window, looking stunned by what he saw. . . .

Which I realized was me, Elise Benton, standing by her parents' huge, ugly, bright green minivan, extending an open cigarette pack to her little sister and—to all appearances—offering her a smoke for the ride.

Derek quickly drove away. Juliana called out a feeble, "See you at the restaurant," and then she and I looked at each other with dismay.

Trust Layla to make me look bad. It was a talent of hers.

Meanwhile, she was clambering happily into the car. "What restaurant?" she asked, poking her head back out.

Juliana told her while I found a trash can to toss the cigarettes into—I didn't want Mom or Dad to find them later—before we headed to Kaitlyn's school.

"Who else is going?" Layla asked. When she heard

53

the names, she bounced up excitedly in her seat. "Whoa! Do you guys know who Derek Edwards is?"

"How do *you* know?" I asked.

"Everyone knows. I mean, he's in *Us Weekly* all the time."

"Really?"

"Well, not *all* the time. But once in a while. With his parents. And this girl I met today was telling me about all the famous kids who go to Coral Tree, and she said he's far and away the most famous. I can't believe you guys are already friends with him. That is so fucking cool!"

"Hey, hey!" Jules said, with a glare in the rearview mirror. "Watch your language, Layla."

"Oh, please. You guys are such prigs. Kids here swear all the time."

"Well, we don't," Jules said. "And if Dad heard you—"

"He won't. I'm not an idiot." She gave another bounce. "Melinda Anton's son!"

Juliana was silent. She was frowning a little and I understood why. "You want to drop us off at home first?" I asked her in a low voice. "You could go on to the restaurant by yourself."

"No, it's okay."

"It might not be."

"It's too late now. She's excited. Hey, Layla?" she said,

54

raising her voice so she could be heard in the backseat.

"What?" Layla had pulled a mini hairbrush out of her bag and was brushing her long dark hair furiously.

"Try to be normal around Derek, okay? Don't bring up his parents or anything like that."

"Don't worry," Layla said. "I know how to be cool."

It took us a while to sign Kaitlyn out of her afterschool program, so the others were already seated at a table eating pizza by the time we got to the restaurant. Let's just say that my idea of cool and Layla's turned out not to be the same. Hers involved audibly whispering, "Is that *him*?" while pointing at Derek, and, upon confirmation, loudly announcing that his mother's picture was on the wall and asking him, "Do they know you're her son? Do you get free food and stuff?"

Kaitlyn proved she was more in Layla's camp than mine when it came to "cool," by accidentally sending a hot, oily garlic roll spinning across the table, where it almost landed in Derek's lap. Then she giggled much too loudly about it even though no one else was amused, and Chelsea, who had been near the line of fire, was shooting her venomous looks.

By the end of the meal, two things were clear:

1. Chase was so crazy about Jules, he didn't seem to notice her youngest sisters were Neanderthals, and

2. Despite Chase's cheerfully optimistic exit line that we should all do this again soon, Derek Edwards didn't seem likely to let himself get trapped into having a meal with the Bentons ever again.

In the car, post–pizza debacle, Kaitlyn happily informed us that she had made a friend at school already, a girl named London, whose parents owned four houses, "if you count their apartment in France."

"Oh, let's count it," I said airily. "I assume they have a place in London, too?"

Kaitlyn furrowed her brow. "I don't think so."

Juliana and I exchanged an amused front-seat look.

"She's an only child, so she doesn't have to share a room in *any* of their houses," Kaitlyn added.

Juliana said, "Don't you think it would be lonely to have such a small family? I love having three sisters."

Kaitlyn twisted her mouth, clearly not sure she agreed. After that meal, I wasn't sure I did, either.

Five

By the time Dad got home, Layla was doing her homework and I was helping Kaitlyn with hers at the wooden farm table in our kitchen—which had made a lot more sense in Amherst, where we'd lived in a former nineteenth-century barn, than here in our sixties-style ranch. Dad trudged in from the garage, shoulders hunched, looking pale and worn-out and older than his fifty-one years. My mother was always trying to get him to go for a run—she seemed to think exercise was the cure for what ailed him—but he always responded in more or less the same way, with a politely impassive look that said, *And why exactly would I want to do that?*

"How'd your first day go?" I asked him after we'd greeted each other.

"Exhausting. And a little worrisome. Take a look at this." He dropped his overstuffed briefcase with a thud onto the linoleum floor and reached into the pocket of his cardigan, which had a big hole right near the shoulder. Great. He had stood in front of every class he taught in that sweater. The man never looked in a mirror.

He pulled out a folded piece of paper and handed it to me. I opened it to reveal two neat columns of names followed by phone numbers. I handed it back. "What is it?"

"A list of all the students who came up to me today to request—make that *insist*—that I contact their math tutors directly. Today's the first day of school—why on earth would these students already have tutors? It's one thing if they start to struggle, but it's like they don't even trust me to teach them in the first place."

"I want a tutor," Layla said. "It would make doing homework so much easier."

"Me too," said Kaitlyn. "If Layla gets one, I get one."

"No daughter of mine will ever have a tutor," Dad said.

"What if we're failing a course?" asked Layla.

His graying eyebrows drew together. "If you fail a single course, young lady, we will pull you out of school and get you a job scrubbing toilets for the rest of your life."

I knew he was teasing her, but he had a scary-good deadpan and Layla's mouth dropped open in outrage. "That's so not fair!"

"Then study hard and get good grades. There's a laziness to this culture that I will not allow my children to succumb to. An intellectual laziness." He added thoughtfully, "Maybe it's all the sunshine—corrodes the brain."

"I like it here," Layla said defiantly. "I mean, I don't like being the new kid, but at least we're finally in a real city where there's more to do than watch the grass grow. And guess who we met today? Melinda Anton's son!"

Dad gazed at her for a moment, the edges of his mouth twitching. "How silly of me to worry that you might succumb to the culture. Thank you for putting my mind at ease on that score." He picked up his briefcase and headed toward his study. "Elise, your mother said she'd be late for dinner. What do you think we should do?"

"We kind of ate already," I said. "Want a slice of pizza?" Chase had insisted we take the extra, since his own family was—as he put it—"allergic to leftovers."

"Would you mind bringing it to my office? I have a lot of work to get through tonight." He left the room, heading toward what my mother referred to—with more hope than sanity—as "the maid's room." It had its own bathroom and hallway and was quieter than any other part of the crowded house, and my dad had instantly nabbed it for his own use when we first moved in two weeks earlier.

I heated up a slice of pizza and brought it to his office, where he sat at his desk, wearily rubbing his temples as he worked on his lesson plans. On my way upstairs, I heard Layla's voice coming from the family room and suspected she was vidchatting.

Up until recently, my sisters and I all had to share one computer, but Juliana and I had successfully lobbied to get our own laptops by quoting the Coral Tree Prep handbook, which said that most high school assignments were posted online. Layla tried to get in on the action, but my parents said she could wait one more year, so she was still sharing the household PC with Kaitlyn.

We had a no-chatting-until-homework-was-done rule, so I headed in to tell her to stop before someone less sympathetic (i.e., Kaitlyn) told on her.

The family room was crammed full with two large sofas, a half dozen side and coffee tables, and several rugs with clashing patterns that overlapped, creating long bumps perfect for tripping us up. We had taken all our furniture with us, and our Amherst house had been twice the size of this one. I stumbled over a rug bump on my way into the room, and Layla looked up, closing the image so I couldn't see what she was doing.

"You know you can't vidchat now," I said. "Not until you've finished your homework."

"I'll get it done. Just give me a minute."

"Layla—"

"Please, Elise." She lowered her voice. "All the girls I know are talking online now. Their parents let them do it whenever they want." She gripped the edge of the computer table. "I have to fit in here. I *have* to. Or I'll die."

"No one dies from not fitting in, Layla. Trust me."

"It's easy for you. You have Juliana. You guys are like the three musketeers." I wasn't sure about the math on that one. "You do everything together and I'm all alone. Kaitlyn's too young—she's useless. And ninth grade is like . . . like some futuristic prison state where everyone's fighting to survive. And if I stand out like some kind of dork, I'm doomed."

She did love her melodrama, my sister. "Don't even try to keep up here," I said. "We don't have the same kind of money, and Mom and Dad are stricter than most of the other parents. You have to find friends who'll accept you the way you are."

"That's what I'm doing," she said. "Really. These girls seem nice. Just let me talk to them for a few more minutes, and then I *promise* I'll do my homework."

"You better." I moved toward the doorway—carefully sidestepping the rug bump this time—and then turned and said, "Look, Layla, vidchatting is no big deal. But don't smoke to fit in. Or do anything else that you know is wrong. That's just stupid."

"I know," she said, her eyes big and brown and a lot like Juliana's. "I won't."

She was either sincere or a very good liar.

Yeah, I know which one, too.

Later that evening, alone in our room doing homework, I told Juliana what Layla had said. "She's always cared too much about fitting in and being popular, but at least back home that just meant being a little cliquish. Here . . ." I ran my finger along the cold metal bed frame: it had been the upper half of a bunk bed in our old house that our parents had separated into twins when we moved because they were worried about earthquakes. "I don't even know what trying to fit in here might involve."

"Do you think we should talk to Mom about her?"

"Nah. Mom has enough going on. And you know how she'd react: we'd all end up living in a prison state. Let's just keep an eye on Layla ourselves."

As if on cue, the door burst open without a knock. "I'm back!" Mom sang out.

Juliana asked her how her day had been.

She adjusted her glasses so they went from tilting too much in one direction to tilting too much the other way. "I have my work cut out for me, that's for sure. I don't think anyone has been enforcing a single rule at that school. I had to confiscate seventeen cell phones today. Seventeen! And then of course the parents were up in arms, calling to complain that they couldn't get in touch with their kids." She shook her head. "You girls have no idea how lucky you are to have parents with real values, who care about raising principled children."

Juliana and I were both silent. We had parents who liked to impose embarrassing restrictions on us. But . . . they cared. There was no denying that.

"So," Mom said, leaning against the doorway, casually retying the bow on her shirt. "That seemed like a nice group of kids you were hanging out with today. They were all so—" She considered her choices before settling on "—interesting." She liked the adjective so much that she immediately used it again. "I'm glad you found such an interesting group of friends so quickly."

"We just ate lunch with them," I said uncomfortably. "That's all."

"That Derek Edwards seems like an especially interesting [*third time*] young man," she said nonchalantly. "Does he talk much about his parents?"

"Not at all," I said. "I don't think he likes to."

"Really? What makes you say that?"

"I don't know. Maybe because people get weird about it." *Like you right now,* I thought.

"Huh," she said. "Well, I hope he realizes that as far as the school administration goes, he's just another student to us."

I shot Juliana a look. She quickly changed the subject. "There's leftover pizza if you're hungry, Mom."

"Oh, did you order in? Try not to make a habit of that." We didn't correct the misunderstanding. Her mind was on a different subject anyway. "There are so many famous people at this school. Did you girls know that James Bryan's kids also go to Coral Tree? And George McGill's and Beatrice Reilly's and—" Before she could finish her recitation of all the celebrities—a couple of whom I'd never even heard of—whose kids were, supposedly, no different from the other students as far as she was concerned, Kaitlyn came rushing in and hurled herself at Mom, wailing, "Layla pushed me!"

"I didn't push her!" yelled Layla, from right behind. "She crossed over onto my side of the room—after I had told her she couldn't—so I just gently made her move away! She's such a baby!"

"IT! WASN'T! GENTLE!" Kaitlyn screamed, turning and standing on her tiptoes so she could shout it right in Layla's face.

My mother sank against the doorjamb. "Do you have any idea how stressful it is to have a hard day at work and then come home to *this* . . . ?"

"It's not my fault," Kaitlyn said, and burst into tears. "She's so mean to me!"

"Could you guys continue this somewhere else?" I asked, with a meaningful nudge at my history binder. Kaitlyn and Layla were always going at it like this, and now that they had to share a room—which they hadn't at our old house—the battles were constant. I was sick of the noise.

Juliana put aside her books and got up from her bed. "I'll take care of it, Mom," she said. "You go eat." My mother thanked her and swiftly disappeared. Jules turned to Kaitlyn. "If you promise not to bother Elise, you can hang out in our room for a little while. Would you like that?"

Kaitlyn happily flung herself on Juliana's bed.

Layla shrugged. "Good riddance," she said, and left.

"Can I sleep in here, too?" Kaitlyn asked, snuggling into a pillow.

"No," I said, but Juliana patted her on the head and said, "We'll see."

A little while later I left to grab a snack and ran into my dad who was exiting the kitchen.

"Just keeping your mother company while she had some dinner," he explained. "She's been telling me stories about the parents at Coral Tree. An entitled group, to say the least—more money than sense, as the saying goes." He hooked his arm in mine. "This is a strange new world we've found ourselves in, my friend."

"No kidding."

"Your mother also told me that you and Juliana are already connected to a very 'in' group of kids. I'm glad you're making friends, Lee-Lee, but don't get too caught up in the social whirl—remember you're working toward a scholarship, something these other kids probably don't have to worry about."

"Don't worry," I said, and grinned at him. "My brain has yet to be corroded by the SoCal sunshine."

"Yet? Let's aim for never, shall we?"

I nodded. "Hey, Dad, I'm basically done with homework for the night. Want to do the crossword puzzle with me?" We liked to do the *New York Times* crossword puzzle together when we had time.

His face lit up. "Absolutely."

A few minutes later we were settled in his office. As I studied the clues, I said, "Thanks for waiting. I know you could do it much faster without me."

"Not true."

I was sitting on the arm of his big office chair. I rested my cheek against his thinning hair. "Dad, it's obvious you have it all done in your head before I even say a word. You give me hints so I *feel* like I'm getting the answers—but it's all you."

He shrugged and smoothed out the paper—the only man left in America who didn't read the news online. "One day, Elise, you're going to outstrip me at everything, even crossword puzzles. And I won't mind one bit."

We had visitors for dinner Thursday night: my mother's brother and his family.

Uncle Mike had a Hollywood-based catering company. Aunt Amy managed the business end. Their daughter, Diana, was three months younger than me.

When we lived in Massachusetts, we saw them only about once a year, but I always liked Diana, who was smart and unpretentious with a dark and self-deprecating sense of humor. We stayed in touch online, but one of the few consolations for having to move my junior year of high school was getting to see her more often.

Within a few minutes of their arrival on Thursday, Mom managed to let drop the fact that Juliana and I had become friends with Melinda Anton and Kyle Edwards's son.

"Not *friends*," I said. "We barely know him."

"You've eaten lunch with him almost every day this week."

So she'd been spying on us. Great. "I eat lunch with Jules who eats with Chase Baldwin—"

"He's Fox Baldwin's son. The music producer," my mother informed the others. "I Googled him, just for fun, and you wouldn't believe the photos and news stories that popped up. He's very well known."

"And Chase and Derek are always together," I continued, trying to ignore my mother's color commentary. "But that doesn't mean Derek's eating with *us*—I don't think he's said two words to me all week."

"If he's sitting across the table from you, he's eating

with you," Mom said firmly.

Diana laughed. "She's got a point, Elise. Plus there's the transitive property: if A eats with B and B eats with C, then A is eating with C."

"I met Kyle Edwards once," said Uncle Mike, scratching at the ever-widening bald spot on his head as if he could uncover the memory below it. "He was at a dinner party I catered."

"What was he like?" Mom asked.

"Vegetarian," he said seriously. "At the time. But these movie stars change their diets constantly. They follow the current fad. Makes my life difficult."

"Yes, they're all on very strict diets until you get a glass of wine into them," said Aunt Amy, who was cheerful and plump but had shrewd eyes that didn't miss a thing. "And then they'll eat anything you put in front of them. Most of them are half-starved."

"We should start a charity," Diana suggested. "Save our poor hungry movie stars."

"We could have a bake sale," I said.

"Or just feed them the cookies directly," said Aunt Amy. "And skip the middleman."

"What do you think, Elise?" asked Diana. "Will your pal Derek Edwards agree to bring home some cookies for his mommy and daddy?"

"Only if they're raw," I said.

* * *

After dinner, Diana and I were on dish duty in the kitchen.

"So, do you like him?" she asked.

"Who?"

She rolled her eyes and put a plate in the dish rack. "Derek Edwards, of course."

I shook my head. "Not really. That friend of his—Chase—seems genuinely into Juliana, and the feeling's clearly mutual—even though Juliana won't admit it yet—so we've gotten stuck together because of that. But Derek's actually kind of a jerk."

"How so?"

"He's really standoffish. He assumes people only want to be friends with him because of his parents."

"Well, he probably has reason for that."

"Maybe. It's still obnoxious."

"Is he cute?"

"Very."

She shoved her chin-length hair behind her ear so she could look sideways at me. "You sure you don't like him?"

"Pretty sure." I covered some leftovers with tinfoil.

"Hmm," she said thoughtfully.

I glanced over my shoulder at her. "What means this 'hmm'?"

"I don't know. Just . . . don't write him off too quickly."

"Why not?"

"Because I'm sure he's not *that* bad . . . and if there's

any chance that you could become friends with Melinda Anton's son, you should do it."

"You're the last person in the world who I would have expected to say something like that."

She laughed. "Relax. I'm not saying you should make out with him because his mother's famous, Elise. Just don't be rude to him." She transferred a stack of dishes from the counter to the sink. "Although if he *asks* you to make out with him—"

"Yeah, that's going to happen."

"I'm joking." She started rinsing off the plates and putting them in the dishwasher. "Seriously, though, my dad would kill for an in with Melinda Anton. Work's slowed down so much for him the last couple of years. All the studios are cutting back—no one's throwing parties anymore. But someone like Melinda Anton will always have money, you know? If she started using him . . ."

"I had no idea," I said. "About your dad and work, I mean. I'm sorry."

"He doesn't like to tell people." She shrugged. "Things are tough all over, right?"

"You wouldn't know it at Coral Tree. Girls come to school in five-hundred-dollar outfits, and the cars they drive are unreal."

"Maybe people who send their kids to private school

are so rich to begin with that they're not affected by the economy."

"Some of them could be getting financial aid, too, I guess." *We* were, even with Mom and Dad's faculty discount. And I assumed Webster was, too, since he had said stuff about not having as much money as other kids at the school. But it wasn't something people talked about. "It's not like you can tell who's getting it and who isn't."

"Anyway, my dad said if things don't get better pretty soon, we may have to move to a less expensive city."

"Like where?"

"I don't know. But I don't want to move." She paused to scrub at a platter way more intently than was necessary. "There's this guy . . ."

"You're dating someone? Diana, that's fantastic."

"Don't get too excited," she said. "He's a total nerd."

"I'm sure he's cute," I said sincerely.

"*I* think so. But it's not like I can be choosy."

"Stop it," I said. "Any guy would be lucky to have you."

"Spoken like a true cousin."

Studying Diana's intelligent and good-natured face as she leaned over to put the platter in the dish drain, I felt a flicker of uneasiness: even she saw advantages to cultivating Derek Edwards as a friend, without knowing

71

or caring much about either his personality or his principles. Even honest, straightforward, decent Diana.

It made me sad for her. It made me sad for him. It made me sad for the world.

And it made me all the more desperate to prove that I wasn't like everyone else that way: I valued people because of who they were deep down, not because of their names or their parents' clout.

And I intended to prove that to myself and everyone around me.

six

"No," I said to Juliana at school on Friday. "No way. *Nein. Nyet. Non.*"

"I'm not going without you."

"Then don't go. I've run out of languages I can say no in, anyway."

"Forget I even asked."

But she looked so disappointed that I groaned and actually surrendered. "I hate it when you're all noble and self-sacrificing! Fine—I'll go. But not happily."

She threw her arms around me. "Thank you, Lee-Lee! You're the best sister ever. I'll call Chase right now."

So that's how I found myself committed to going with Jules and Chase to a party thrown by Jason Bigelow, the captain of the lacrosse team, a guy I'd never even met.

It was Layla who first alerted the rest of the family to the fact that a stretch limousine had pulled up in front of our house on Saturday night. "Oh my God, oh my God!" she squealed, looking out the front window. "It's like a block long! You guys are so friggin' lucky!" All her squeals brought my parents and Kaitlyn running into the hallway to see.

"This is exactly what I'm talking about," my father said as Juliana and I arrived downstairs. "This kind of excess. Please, girls, remember that this isn't normal, okay?"

"They know that," Mom said. "Our girls have good heads on their shoulders." And then she strode out the door.

Juliana gasped and we both lunged for her, but she was already charging down the walkway to where the chauffeur was opening the door of the long, dark car. Chase emerged, gracefully unfolding his slender body. His dark gray khakis and blue-and-white-striped oxford shirt were very collegiate and blessedly clean-cut, given that my parents were watching. "Good evening, Dr. Gardiner," he said, holding out his hand and shaking hers. "Thank you for trusting me with your daughters tonight."

My mother smiled at that. She liked polite young men. "I appreciate that very much, Mr. Baldwin. And whom do you have in the car with you?"

"My sister and my friend." He called over his shoulder,

"Come out and say hi, guys."

Chelsea exited the limo with a very put-upon expression on her face. She was wearing extremely tight blue jeans and a corset top that revealed a lot of slender arm, white shoulder, and bright pink bra strap. I was afraid my mother might say something disapproving, but—for better or for worse—her attention was completely focused on the other passenger coming out of the limo. "Mr. Edwards!" she exclaimed with genuine delight. "My girls didn't tell me you were coming, too!"

Ten moderately mortifying minutes later, we were on our way. My mom had insisted on thanking Derek over and over again for picking us up in his limo—she didn't seem to absorb his muttered, "It's not mine; it's Chase's dad's." She was still thanking him when we were all climbing into the back of it.

As we left her behind on the sidewalk—cheerfully waving—the five of us sank down on the soft leather benches that ran both lengths of the elongated car body. Chase and Jules were next to each other, of course. I was on Juliana's other side, which put me opposite Derek Edwards, whose long legs took up all the available in-between space. I had to curl my own legs sideways or risk rubbing knees.

Chelsea was glued to Derek's side, which didn't

surprise me since I was convinced she had the world's biggest crush on him. I wasn't as sure about his feelings toward her. He seemed comfortable having her around, but I wasn't seeing a ton of romantic interest there.

On the other hand, the guy was impossible to read in almost every way. For all I knew, he was madly head over heels in love with Chelsea Baldwin, but was so repressed and weird you couldn't tell. For all I knew, he was gay.

I was still wearing the sweater I'd put on over my tank top to make it past my mother, and which completely ruined the look I was going for. I started to pull it off, but it got stuck halfway down my arms. I was twisting around awkwardly, trying to wriggle free, when I felt a hand tug the sleeves down and off me. I looked up. Derek Edwards had leaned forward to help me. "Thanks," I said.

The sound of a cell phone vibrating broke the awkward silence. Derek swiftly extracted a phone from his right hip pocket and squinted down at the screen. He read something before texting back a response, skillfully dancing his thumbs on the touchscreen.

Meanwhile, Chelsea had snuggled closer to his side and was craning her neck over his shoulder in an effort to read what he was writing. "Who're you texting?"

"My sister."

"Oh my God! Georgia! I haven't heard from her in

ages! I miss hanging out with her *so* much. Tell her I miss hanging out with her, will you?"

"Tell her yourself."

"She's so lucky to be out of here!"

Why did that cause such a miserable expression to cross Derek's face? I could see it clearly from where I was sitting. But Chelsea was oblivious. She went blithely on. "Will she come home for Thanksgiving?"

"Probably."

"Make sure she saves lots of time for me. I miss her so much."

"Really?" He finished texting and leaned sideways so he could stick the phone back in his pocket. "I didn't think you guys were that close. You're not even in the same grade."

"Brothers never notice anything."

"I didn't know you had a sister," I said to Derek. "She doesn't go to Coral Tree?"

"She did, but this year she switched to boarding school."

"Any special reason?"

Derek's eyes flitted across my face, and then he looked down at his hands and said tonelessly, "Coral Tree's a mediocre school academically. My parents thought she needed a place that was more challenging." It sounded like something he had memorized.

"And it's getting worse by the hour," Chelsea said.

"No offense to your mother," she added, just to make sure I got the point that she was being offensive to my mother.

I ignored her. "What about you?" I asked Derek. "Why didn't your parents take *you* out of Coral Tree?"

He shrugged. "I'm a mediocre student. Coral Tree's fine for me."

"Don't believe it!" Chelsea said. "Derek's, like, the smartest kid in his class."

"How would *you* know?" he asked. "This is the first time we've ever had a class together."

"Everyone says so."

"Well, I'm not. Not even close."

"But why a boarding school?" I pursued, genuinely curious. "There are other college prep schools here in L.A. Some really good ones. So why—"

He shifted on the bench and pointed out the window. "Look, the Getty Museum monorail."

Chelsea obediently gazed out the window. But I was more curious than ever. Derek Edwards was not the kind of guy who went around pointing enthusiastically at trains. He just didn't want to answer my questions.

Chelsea split from the rest of us as soon as we entered the loud, noisy, crowded party house.

No, wait—I take that back. It wasn't right away, because first she tugged on Derek's arm and said, "Want to dance?" and he said, "You know I don't dance," and then she said, "Help me find the bar," and he said, "It's over there," and then she said, "Come get a drink with me," and he said, "I'm not thirsty," and then she said, "Let's go see the indoor pool," and he said, "I've seen it," and *then* she gave up and headed toward a group of her friends, although not without one last overly loud and enthusiastic, "Bye, Derek! Come find me later!" which was clearly intended for her friends' ears, so they'd all think she and Derek had come together, I assumed. Which they had—but not in *that* way.

"Should we get something to drink?" Chase asked right after she'd gone.

"Yeah, I'd kill for a Coke," Derek said, and led the way toward the bar he had pointed out a second earlier to Chelsea.

Okay, so he definitely wasn't interested in her romantically.

The bar was the real thing, an ornately carved wooden counter with a built-in sink and (locked) wine storage unit behind it. I had never seen one in a house in real life, only in TV shows and movies.

Then again, the whole house was like nothing I'd seen before. Chelsea had made several deprecating comments in the car about how annoying it was that we had to trek all the way to the "sucky Valley," so I had expected to end up at some nasty little tract house, not at an enormous gated estate.

I was relieved to see nothing alcoholic on the bar—no need to lie to my mother, who always warned us to leave any party immediately if we saw anyone drinking. I wondered sometimes if she was deliberately naive about this stuff. I mean, she'd been in high school administration for more than a decade. She had to have some sense of reality, right?

I was always honest about my own behavior—I never drank alcohol. But if I told my parents the entire truth—that almost everyone *else* drank beer at parties—they wouldn't let me or my sisters go anywhere ever again.

Mom and Dad loved to say, "We trust you to behave appropriately," and then not trust us at all. I didn't want to deceive my parents. But they didn't leave me much choice.

Chase saw me studying the contents of the bar. "It's all soda," he confirmed. "Jason has this deal with his parents: he can throw as many parties as he likes so long as he doesn't serve alcohol." He added in a low voice, "He doesn't necessarily stop people from *bringing* it, of course. So, if you guys want something like that, I can ask around. . . ."

"No, thanks," Juliana said quickly. "I'm happy with Diet Coke."

"Me too," I said. "It's the Official Drink of Girls."

"Boys too. I love the stuff." Chase seemed relieved

that we'd turned down his offer, which made me like him even more.

Derek pulled the tab on a can of regular Coke.

Then Chase said to Juliana with über-casualness, "Want to see the rest of this place? They have an amazing aquarium in one of the back rooms."

I almost giggled. Talk about a line. I realized Derek's lips were twitching too, and our eyes briefly met in shared amusement.

"Elise?" Jules said uncertainly.

"You go ahead. I'm fine here." I wasn't really—I didn't know anyone else—but the sooner Chase got some time alone with her, the sooner we could leave. I hoped.

"You can come with us," she offered.

I shot her a *Give the guy a break* look. Out loud, I said, "I'll catch up with you in a minute."

"Sounds good," Chase said, and hustled her away. I watched them as they made their way through the crowd, their heads bent close together, his hand lingering on her arm.

"So," Derek said from right next to me. I jumped. I had forgotten about him. "Want to—" He stopped. He seemed uncertain how to finish the sentence.

"It's okay," I said. "You don't have to babysit me."

"You probably don't know that many people here."

"That's what parties are for, right? To get to know people?"

"I don't know what they're for, to be honest. I'm not a fan of them." He did look pretty uncomfortable as he clutched his Coke to his chest, his eyes darting warily around the room.

The irony was, of course, that almost anyone there would happily have hung with him. The girls would have danced with him, and the boys would have dragged him off to do . . . whatever boys do at parties. But he pretty much made himself unapproachable: he avoided eye contact and barely acknowledged anyone who tried to greet him.

"Why'd you come tonight?" I asked abruptly.

"Chase wanted to."

"You always do whatever he wants?"

"Pretty much. He's more like a brother than a friend at this point."

"I know what you mean. Juliana's just like a sister to me."

"Now that's a little weird," he said, with that brief shadow of a smile I'd seen once or twice before. There was a short pause. "You play Ping-Pong?"

"Not well. But I like it."

"Perfect." He put his drink down on the bar. "I'll beat you. I like winning."

I put mine down, too. "Where to?"

"Downstairs. They have a rec room in the basement."

We threaded a path through the crowd in the living

room and then through another much darker room, where loud music throbbed while couples ground their bodies together. It was suffocatingly hot, and I was glad I had left my sweater in the car . . . uh, limo.

One girl was dancing all by herself, swaying to what must have been a beat inside her own head, because her movements in no way matched the one we could hear. Her eyes were closed—the better to hear that internal tune, I guess—and as we tried to slip by, she suddenly bobbed right in front of me, forcing me to step back so quickly that I knocked into someone behind me. My rebound from *that* sent me tripping over a random foot, and I almost hit the floor, but Derek quickly grabbed my arm and steadied me before I could fall.

Then, without saying anything, he slid his hand down to clasp my wrist, which he continued to hold as he navigated our way through the crowd. There was nothing romantic about it—he was just leading me through the press of people and probably figured (with undeniable justification) that I'd hurt myself if he didn't keep a grip on me. But I was very aware of his warm fingers against my skin and ducked my head, relieved no one could see me blush in the darkened room.

We emerged from the dance room into a back hallway that was quieter but even darker. "This way," Derek said, and steered me toward the top of a stairway. He suddenly pulled me against his side, and it took me a moment to realize he had once again saved me—this time from falling over the extended legs of a kid who was sitting on the floor, his back against the wall, a girl curled up on his lap, her lips plastered against his, his hands snaking down her jeans. I felt a jolt of embarrassment as we crept around them and headed down the stairs—for them because they were doing stuff in public no one should do in public, and also for us because we could see them doing it. Not that they noticed us.

Derek released my hand without a word as we stepped down into the most enormous room I'd ever seen in a private home. Only the words "airplane hangar" could do it justice. It was carpeted and lined with floor-to-ceiling velvet curtains, probably to muffle the noise currently being generated by the use of a pool table, a Ping-Pong table, and, at the far end of the room, a wall-sized entertainment console containing a gigantic flat-screen TV and several video game systems.

This was clearly where all the guys who didn't have dates had ended up—and, given how many of them were passionately watching or playing video games, I don't think there was any huge mystery to their lack of girlfriends.

Derek headed toward the Ping-Pong table, which two guys were already using.

All Derek said was, "When you're done, let us know," and instantly one skinny, zit-scarred player said, "It's all yours," and offered up his paddle. "Let's go, Jay," he called to his short and slightly chubby opponent, who obediently surrendered his paddle to Derek in turn. Grinning and nodding, the first kid led his friend over toward the TV. As they moved off, I could hear him whisper, "You know who that is, right?"

"Does that always happen to you?" I asked Derek as he handed me a paddle.

"What?" He moved around to the other end of the table.

"Do people always let you have whatever you want when you want it?"

"What do you mean?"

"You know. Because your parents are famous. Those guys wouldn't have stopped playing for anyone else."

"Whatever," he said. "I didn't ask them to. I can't control what other people do." He tossed the ball in the air and caught it. "Are we going to play or not?"

"I'm really bad at this," I said. "I'm not sure I was clear enough about that earlier."

He cocked his head at me. "Why do I have the feeling I'm being hustled?"

"Don't be silly," I said. Then, "Of course, if you want to put a little wager on it . . ."

"Loser has to sit next to Chelsea on the way home," he said, and served.

We played for the next half hour. Derek was much better than me, so it was a totally uneven game, but he didn't seem to mind. He even came around the table at one point to show me how to hit the ball backhand—I had a bad habit of shifting so I could always use my forehand.

"Like this," he said and got behind me and put his arm around mine so he could guide me through the motion. I glanced up at him as he gently glided my hand back and forth. His face was close to mine, and I quickly looked back down again. It was the proximity, I told myself. I wasn't used to being that close to any guy. The catch in my throat had nothing to do with him specifically.

But when he went back to the other side and waited for me to serve, my fingers were suddenly clumsy. I dropped the ball and had to squat down ungracefully to grab it from under the table.

At least I hadn't worn a miniskirt.

It got harder and harder to remember that Derek was this screwed-up celebrity brat as our game went on. He was livelier and more relaxed than I'd ever seen him before. He even flashed a real smile now and then, not just the creepy ghost one.

"You really *are* bad at this," he said, after I hit the ball so hard in a downward motion that it bounced straight up, almost to the ceiling, then back down again—still on my side. But his tone was teasing, not critical.

"Told you." I tossed the ball to him and he served it gently, right down the middle. I easily hit it back. "Now you're just patronizing me," I said.

"Do you prefer this?" He slammed the ball at me as hard as he could, and I shrieked and curled my body up, hands instinctively rising to protect my face.

"Patronize me!" I said, peeking through my fingers. "Patronize me, please!"

"If you say so . . ."

I retrieved the ball from the floor. "No wonder people play Ping-Pong," I said as I stood back up. "It's like doing squats."

"Yeah, that's usually not such a big part of the game." He gave me an easy serve, but I still missed the return. "Hey, I have a question for you," he said when I had retrieved the ball and tossed it back to him.

"What's that?"

He raised his paddle but halted in that position. "Do you smoke?"

"Smoke? Cigarettes, you mean?"

"Yeah."

"Never," I said. "Why do you ask?"

"It's just . . . I saw you giving one to your little sister. I've been wondering."

I suddenly realized what he was talking about. "Oh, you mean in the parking lot the first day of school! That was *her* pack—it had fallen out of her pocket. And I wasn't giving it to her; I was reaming her out for having it in the first place." I laughed. "You should have seen the expression on your face as you drove by us."

"I was a little shocked," he admitted.

"Yeah, I can see why. But I swear I was confiscating it."

"I believe you. You don't smell like an ashtray."

"Cool," I said. "I passed the sniff test without even knowing I was taking it."

"So Layla smokes? A little young, isn't she?"

"She claimed she was holding the pack for a friend."

"Hmm," he said.

"Exactly." I turned the paddle around in my hands, gently stroking my fingers over the pebbled surface of its face. "Every big family has to have a problem child, right?"

"She's the one in yours?"

"Well, it's certainly not Juliana," I said. "And Kaitlyn's pretty normal."

"I nominate you for the position. You seem like a troublemaker to me."

"Me?" I said. "I'm a saint."

"Saint Elise, huh?"

"Yes, and don't you forget it. Are you ever going to serve, or are you just going to stand there posing?"

He served, but he continued to go so easy on me that I caught up to him.

"Okay," he said when the score was nineteen to nineteen. "I'm facing a bit of a dilemma here. The gentlemanly thing to do would be to let you win. But we're playing for high stakes. I'm not sure I'm willing to make the sacrifice."

"Ah, you see?" I said. "I've lulled you into a false sense of security. This is when I put the blitz on and destroy you."

"Really?" he said, and slammed the ball at me.

"No!" I said, cowering again. "I can't blitz! I don't even know what a blitz is!"

Five seconds later, he'd beaten me. We met halfway around the table and shook hands. "I'm not trying to get out of the bet or anything," I said, "but there is a slight logistical problem I should point out."

"What's that?"

He was still holding my hand. I had to clear my throat. "I'll try my best to sit next to Chelsea, but we both know she's going to be trying even harder to sit next to you— and I think her will may be stronger than mine."

He gave my hand a squeeze that could have been

a reprimand or something else entirely. "Deal with it, Saint Elise. You made a promise."

"You're just hoping to see a catfight."

He shook his head. "Oh, please. Just because I'm a guy, you think I like catfights."

"You mean you don't?"

He grinned. I swear: *Derek Edwards grinned.* "I didn't say that."

The guys we had originally bounced from the Ping-Pong table must have seen us put down our paddles, because they were drifting back toward us. Derek released my hand.

"What should we do now?" he asked, like it was a given we'd stick together.

"I don't know." I glanced around the rec room. Nothing inspired me. "Let's go back upstairs and see what's going on up there."

The second we moved away, the boys darted forward and grabbed our paddles.

"Thanks for letting us play," I called over my shoulder, and they bobbed their heads in a kind of salute.

"I should probably find Juliana at some point," I said as we headed up the stairs. "Except—"

"What?"

"I'm not convinced she wants to be found."

"I know what you mean. I've never seen Chase so—" He stopped. At first I thought he just didn't want to finish what he was saying, but then I realized he was staring up the steps, where a long, angular figure was tromping rapidly down toward us. Webster Grant.

"Hi!" I said, happy to see a friendly face in a house full of strangers.

"Elise Benton! My long-lost cousin!" He took my hand and pressed it warmly. He was wearing a light blue polo shirt that matched the color of his eyes. "Hey, Derek!" he said. "How's it going, buddy?"

Derek's smile had vanished, leaving his face cold and rigid. He ignored Webster, just brushed past him and continued trudging up the stairs with heavy, deliberate steps.

"Um, good-bye?" I called out to his retreating back.

He looked over his shoulder at me. "Aren't you coming?"

"Kind of saying hello to a friend here?"

"I'll be upstairs." He kept going and vanished into the hallway above.

I stared after him. "A little moody, isn't he?" I tried to sound lighthearted but I was truly stunned at Derek's sudden transformation. We'd been having fun together. At least, I thought we'd been.

Webster patted me on the arm consolingly. "Well, you can't say I didn't warn you. How'd you end up hanging out with him anyway?"

"We came in the same car. My sister and Chase

wanted to come to this together, and we both tagged along. And then we played Ping-Pong—"

"Not pool? I always assumed he was a billiards man—I mean, it's so handy the way he keeps a stick up his—"

"Hey, hey," I said, laughing. "That's Melinda Anton's wittle baby boy you're talking about and don't you forget it."

"Oh, are we allowed to forget it? I thought there were laws against that." He glanced around. "So where were you on your way to, young Elise, and may I escort you there since your companion appears to have abandoned you? His loss, I might add. Which I'm hoping will turn out to be my gain."

"I'd like to find my sister. I'm ready to head home, but she's my ride. Well, the Baldwins' limo is literally my ride, but she's my connection to it."

Webster whistled. "A limo? How very West Side of you. What's it like living the good life?"

"The ride is smooth, but the company stinks," I said, and he grinned. I felt slightly guilty. It hadn't been that bad, had it? I mean, Chase was a nice guy and Derek . . .

I didn't know what to think about Derek.

"In that case," Webster said, neatly pivoting on the balls of his feet so we could head up the stairs together, "how about I take you home? I ain't got no limo, but I can offer you a ride in one smoking hot Chevy Aveo. It's small, it's slow, I bought it used, and if you wanted to find a cheaper car, you'd have to go to India. . . . But it works and it's all mine."

"I don't know." I pretended to be torn. "The limo had carpeting. And snacks!"

We had reached the top of the stairs. He stopped and looked at me. "Seriously, Elise, I'd be happy to take you home. Honored, even."

I thought it would be kind of nice to be alone in a car with Webster Grant and his light blue eyes, especially since it felt like I'd basically been dumped by everyone I'd come with. "I just have to check with my sister. I promised to stay by her side tonight."

Webster laughed. The guy had the greatest laugh— it bubbled up from deep inside his chest and instantly made you want to join in. "I hate to tell you this, but you failed at that job."

"Hey, *she* abandoned *me*."

"Well, there you go. You don't owe her anything."

I touched his arm. "You said when we had more time, you'd tell me why you and Derek stopped being friends." I'd been wanting to bring that up again since Derek had walked away.

"Oh, right." He made a face. "Honestly, it's not much of a story. The short version is that his little sister—" He stopped and started again. "Derek and I used to hang out sometimes, and she—" He laughed sheepishly. "It's embarrassing to say, but she kind of got a crush on me. I didn't even realize it. I mean, I was nice to her, the way you are to a friend's little sister, and I even gave her a couple of rides home from school. Which turned out to be a mistake, because then she said something about how we were 'going out' to Derek. He didn't even ask me what the truth was—just went ballistic."

"What do you mean?"

"He wouldn't talk to me, wouldn't let me explain, wouldn't let Georgia so much as say hi to me anymore."

"Sounds way over the top," I said.

"He's just super-protective of her. To be fair, I think Georgia made it worse by getting all Romeo and Juliet about it even though it was nothing like that. You haven't met her yet, but the girl's a little . . ." He hesitated. "Oh God, I don't want to be mean about her. She's sweet and all. She's just . . . not all there. Which I guess is why she made up this whole fantasy in the first place."

"That's kind of sad," I said.

"No kidding. I couldn't be mad at her—I just felt sorry for her. But it ruined my friendship with Derek." He swung up onto the landing. "Come on. Let's go." He pointed to a poster on the wall as I followed him. "Look."

It was dark so I had to move closer to see it. "*Ship of Cool?* I saw that movie!"

"Everyone saw that movie. It was the second biggest

hit of 2007. And guess whose studio made it?"

"Whose?"

"Jason's mother's." He swept his arm in a circle. "This is the house that *Ship of Cool* built."

As we moved into the dark upstairs hallway, I noticed that the couple Derek and I had stepped over were still making out. No, wait . . . on closer inspection (but not too close), it was a different couple.

"I have a confession to make," Webster said, after we had tiptoed our way around them.

"Uh-oh."

"It's not easy for me to tell you this, but it's important that our relationship be built on a foundation of perfect honesty." He halted and bent down to put his mouth close to my ear. His breath felt warm against my skin and I shivered a little—and hoped he didn't notice. "When I said the car was all mine, I lied. It's actually my parents'. It's our family's one car, and it was only because my mother has the flu that I managed to score it this evening." He took a step back. "Think you can forgive me?"

"I'm not about to criticize anyone's car situation. Have you seen the Benton-mobile?"

"No, why?"

"Three words." I counted them off on my fingers. "Green. Old. Minivan."

Webster gave a mock shudder. "Good God, woman," he said. "Lower your voice. You could get thrown out of a party like this for less than that."

"Exactly."

"You know what?" he said, taking my arm. "You and I had better stick together."

I smiled right into those blue eyes and said, "It's us against them."

We made our way through the dance room. Crazy swaying girl was still there, but I successfully dodged her this time, and we made it back safely to the living room, which was even hotter and more crowded than before.

"Let's grab something to drink for the road," Webster said, raising his voice so I could hear him over the noise. We moved toward the bar. "What do you feel like?"

"Diet Coke," I shouted back.

"Ah, the hard stuff!" We made it to the bar, and Webster reached for a bottle of Diet Coke.

That's when things got weird.

Over Webster's shoulder, I could see a bunch of guys pushing through the crowd, heading toward us. They were all big, with the broad shoulders and overdeveloped biceps that basically functioned as a *Hello, I'm a Jock* name tag.

Derek was one of them. In fact, he was leading the way, his face grim, his shoulders hunched forward, and his arms curving down, the way they do when guys want to give the impression that their muscles are almost *too* big. He walked right by me like I wasn't there and grabbed the bottle out of Webster's hand. "Time to go, Grant."

"Excuse me?" The polite smile on Webster's face made me think maybe he really hadn't heard. Other people must have, though: there was a perceptible lowering of voices all around us.

Derek put the Diet Coke back on the bar and gestured to another guy to come forward. This guy had overgrown wavy red hair and the widest shoulders I'd ever seen. Too bad he didn't have a neck—just a big head that sprung directly from the middle of those enormous shoulders. He said in a growl, "I don't remember inviting you to my house. Leave. Now."

"*What?*" I exclaimed, but Webster gave a resigned shrug and said, "A couple of people told me it was an open party. Sorry. I was on my way out, anyway." He turned to me. "Let's go."

"This is nuts," I said.

He gave a short laugh. "I've been thrown out of better places than this."

I looked at Derek. "What's going on?" He didn't bother to meet my eyes, just kept glaring at Webster. "Why are you guys acting like such jerks?" I asked.

Jason heard that. "Who are you? You come with Grant?"

"No, but I'm leaving with him," I said hotly. "The hospitality here sucks."

Derek stepped forward. "She came with me, actually. She's Juliana's sister."

"Juliana?" Jason repeated blankly.

"The new girl," Derek explained, and Jason nodded, recognition dawning. "Oh, her."

"Don't you think this is a little much?" I asked Derek, who didn't reply.

"It's okay, Elise. No big deal. Let's just go." Webster crooked his elbow toward me, and I threaded my arm through his.

"You can't go," Derek said, addressing me directly for the first time. "Your sister is expecting you to come home with us."

"Tell her I made other plans," I hissed. But then I heard my name being called.

Juliana was rushing over, Chase right behind. "What's going on?" she asked.

"Give me a second," I said to Webster, releasing his arm.

"Don't know if I have one," he said, with a wary look at the hostile faces surrounding us.

"Yeah, okay. Go ahead and I'll meet you out front."

"I'll wear a carnation in my lapel so you'll recognize me." Amazing that he could still crack a joke under these circumstances.

He sauntered calmly across the floor, apparently

indifferent to the people whispering all around him. Once he had closed the front door behind him, Jason's gang melted into the crowd, their community service completed for the night.

I dragged Juliana over to a quiet corner of the room.

"What was that all about?" she asked. "Who was that?"

"This guy I'm friends with—he just got thrown out of the party. Because of Derek."

"Why? What did he do?"

"Nothing. He didn't do anything."

She tossed her hands up in the air. "I don't understand!"

"I don't either. All I know is that Derek has it in for Webster, and of course everyone does whatever Melinda Anton's son says, so—" I shrugged irritably. "It's all weird and annoying, and I'm getting a ride home from Webster. You want to come with us?"

"What about Chase?"

"Just tell him you got another ride."

She looked down at the floor. "I don't want to." No surprise there.

"Fine. I'll see you later." I turned to go.

"You'll go straight home, right? Mom and Dad will freak if I get home and you're not with me."

"I'll text you once I know what I'm doing."

I headed toward the front door, confused and a little overwhelmed. The evening had started off badly, then had gotten better, then had turned strange . . . and now I was leaving with a guy I hadn't arrived with. Not my usual m.o. But as far as car companions went, I was trading up. Better to ride in a lousy little car with someone fun than in a limo with a jerk.

I let the door swing closed behind me and looked around. Webster wasn't anywhere in sight.

That was weird: I thought he said he'd wait for me. I walked down to the open gargantuan metal gate and looked up and down the street. There were no sidewalks in this neighborhood, just big, gated houses and the dark street that divided them.

To my relief, a tall figure moved out of the shadows and came toward me. I went to meet him, but my greeting died on my lips as he emerged into the street lamp's glow. It wasn't Webster at all.

It was Derek Edwards.

"Hi," he said.

"Where's Webster?"

"He's gone."

"What do you mean? He's supposed to take me home."

He shook his head. "He drove off a minute ago."

"You're lying."

"No," he said, so calmly I believed him.

"Did you tell him to leave without me?"

"More or less."

"Why?"

Derek was silent a moment. Then he said, "Webster's not a good person. You don't want to hang out with him."

"He's not the one knocking into people and throwing them out of parties!"

"Why are you in such a hurry to be on his side?" Derek kicked at a piece of metal lying on the side of the road and, without looking up, said, "Because he's funny? Because he says bad things about me?"

"He doesn't say anything bad about anyone!" I hated how shrill my voice was getting, but I couldn't stop it. I felt totally confused about what was going on, and I hate feeling confused. "That's where you're wrong. He's only ever been nice about you. He likes you. He understands that you—" I stopped.

"What does he understand?" he asked sharply.

"That things are weird for you," I said. "That having famous parents makes you a little . . . you know . . . paranoid." I tried to say it gently but realized too late that a word like *paranoid* comes out sounding pretty harsh whether you want it to or not.

"That's what Webster says about me?"

"Yeah, well, it's kind of true, isn't it?" I said, speaking

rapidly to cover my discomfort. "I mean, the first time I met you I didn't even know who your parents were, but everyone seemed to assume I did. And then every time anyone even mentions your parents, you act like they're invading your privacy or being rude or something. It's impossible to be normal around you."

He recoiled. "Is that your opinion or Webster Grant's?"

"It's the *truth*," I said. "Ask anyone—only no one will tell you because they all want to be friends with you."

"What makes you the noble exception? No interest in being friends?"

Was he angry? His voice was quiet but heavy with sarcasm and something else—disappointment, maybe?

"I *am* interested in being friends," I said. "But not because of who your parents are. And not as much as I was before I saw you acting like a jerk to a guy who hadn't done you any harm."

"You don't know anything about it."

"Yes, I do—he told me you guys used to be friends, and then there was this thing with your little sister . . ."

He shook his head. "He didn't tell you everything."

"Look," I said, trying to be conciliatory. "I get that you feel protective of your little sister. Layla's always getting in trouble and I try—"

He cut me off. "My sister isn't like yours," he said coldly. "She's a good kid."

I drew my head back. "What exactly are you saying?"

"Nothing. Just don't assume my sister is anything like yours."

I dug my nails into my palms, furious at how condescending and critical he sounded. But I tried to stay calm. "Fine," I said. "Whatever. Let's say you're justified in disliking Webster—and that's a pretty big leap, but let's just say it for the moment. Does that also give you the right to kick him out of parties and keep me from getting a ride with him?"

"I did you a favor."

"Oh, please," I said. "I can make my own choices."

"Webster Grant knows how to get people to like him—"

"Yeah," I said. "He's pleasant and outgoing and friendly. What a jerk. Why can't everyone be rude and standoffish? That's so much better. So much classier."

Derek took in a quick breath and then let it out in an angry puff. "Forget it," he said. "You're determined to think I'm a jerk, no matter what I say. And frankly, I'm not that high on you either right now. I thought you'd be a better judge of character." He raised his hands and let them drop. "Let's just go find Chase and your sister and get the hell out of here."

"I'm not going with you guys," I said. "Not now."

"Really, Elise? How exactly are you planning to get home?"

Good question. It's not like I had other options. Derek knew it and I knew it. "Come on," he said in a gentler tone. "The sooner we find the others, the sooner you'll be home."

"I'll wait here." I crossed my arms and leaned against the street lamp.

"Suit yourself." He walked away and strode through the huge metal gate.

seven

The ride home was about as awkward as you could get.

Juliana's eyes kept straying anxiously over to where I sat opposite her, all curled in on myself.

Chelsea sat between me and Derek. As we'd gotten into the limo, I'd remembered our Ping-Pong wager, but neither Derek nor I brought it up. We were both being stiffly polite but didn't meet each other's eyes or address each other directly.

When her first few attempts at engaging Derek in conversation failed, Chelsea yawned and stretched and said a little too loudly, "God, I'm tired." She daintily laid her head on Derek's shoulder. "This is nice," she said with a contented sigh. She fluttered her eyelashes up at him and then let her eyes close, thus missing the annoyed look he shot her.

I caught it, though, and my eyes met his, briefly and unintentionally. We both quickly looked away again. Then he twitched his shoulders with a sudden violence that made Chelsea's neck bounce. She lifted her head and said, "Hey!"

"Can you not do that, please?" he said.

She made a face, but shifted back into an upright position. "You're not nice," she said, with what I'm sure was supposed to be an adorable and irresistible pout.

"So I've been told." Those were the last words he spoke for the rest of the drive to our house.

When we pulled up, I opened the car door before we'd even come to a full stop and headed up the front walkway with one quick and muttered good-bye tossed over my shoulder. I figured Juliana could thank them for both of us. I wasn't in the mood.

My father must have heard the car because he opened the door for me. "Did you have a good time?" he asked as he let me in.

"Not really."

"I'm sorry to hear that," he said cheerfully. "You're like me, Elise," he added. "You don't want to be gadding about, going to silly parties, making inane conversation with shallow people. You're happier curled up at home with a good book."

I almost laughed at that. Me, like my dad? No way.

He was a social recluse—almost never left the house except for work.

How could I be like him? I was young. I was a girl. I had long hair and liked to wear pretty clothes and go out at night. I *loved* my dad, but I was nothing like him.

But then I felt a flutter of panic. I had his genes. What if they were just lurking in me, waiting to be expressed? He was always telling me that I was the most like him of his four daughters. Maybe someday in the future, I would be the one puttering around in an old cardigan with stretched-out pockets, carrying cups of strong tea to my office where I'd read books and journals hour after hour and complain about how standards were being compromised.

I had a sudden violent desire to run out and get a tattoo.

My mother came bustling into the foyer. "Oh, good, you're home, Elise. Juliana outside?" She opened the front door, just as Layla came dashing down the stairs, wearing her pajama bottoms and a sweatshirt.

"I want to see the limo," she said and darted out the open door.

"Layla!" I called and headed after her, terrified she'd say something embarrassing to Derek. Right now, that would be unbearable.

She had reached the curb by the time I caught up to her. "Can I see inside?" she asked Chase who was standing there, saying good-bye to Juliana. "I've never been in one before." Before he could respond, she had crawled through the door. I could hear her "Hey, Derek! Nice limo!" and his weary "It's not mine."

"There's a whole cabinet of food in here! With Oreos! And a TV! Look—DVDs!" Layla stuck her head out the limo door. "Mom, you have to see this. It's incredible!"

I hadn't realized that Mom had followed us out, but there she was, right behind me. She smiled, a little patronizingly. "Yes, I know, Layla. I saw it earlier." She stooped and peered inside. "Hi, kids! Did you have a good time? No drinking, right? Who needs alcohol to have fun?"

"Mom, they have to get going," I said, desperate to stop her before she launched into an entire PSA. "Come *on*, Layla." I hauled her out of the limo.

To my surprise, Derek followed her out onto the sidewalk. "I think this is yours," he said and handed me the cardigan sweater I had shrugged off hours earlier and completely forgotten about.

"Oh, right. Thanks." I accepted the sweater without meeting his eyes.

Layla tugged at his arm. "You have to take me for a ride one day. It would be so cool to show up at a rave in this!"

"Layla!" my mother said. "What do you know about raves? She's very advanced for her age," she told Derek.

108

"I worry about it sometimes, but, really, what can you do?"

"Tie her to a tree," I muttered and I could have sworn I heard a smothered laugh, but when I glanced at Derek, his face was blank.

"Please thank your parents for the use of their limo," Mom said to him.

"It's not theirs," I said. "It's the Baldwins'."

"Anyway, good-bye!" said Juliana, clearly as eager as I was for this farewell to end. Chase and Derek quickly—and with some relief—said good night and disappeared into the limo.

Mom leaned in. "Come back soon and stay awhile!" she said gaily. "Both of you are welcome anytime. And your families, too, of course. We just set up a croquet course in our backyard. It's a little cramped but it's fun!"

I reached around her and slammed the door shut.

"So what was going on at the party with Derek and that Webster guy?" Juliana asked when we were both back in our room.

I told her the little I knew.

She furrowed her brow, clearly trying to make sense of it. "Derek thinks there was something weird going on with Webster and his sister?"

"I guess. Webster says she just had a crush on him."

"Maybe the truth lies somewhere in the middle," she

suggested. "Maybe Webster flirted a little with the sister and it bothered Derek."

"Webster's chatty and outgoing, so it could easily come across as flirtatious—but he's also obviously harmless. And if that's the case, Derek way overreacted tonight: he threw him out of the party and then made him leave without me. Don't you think that's pretty bad?"

"Well," she said, "there may be more to the story we don't know."

"You just want to side with Derek because he's Chase's friend." She didn't rush to deny it. "Did Chase say anything about Webster to you?"

"We didn't have a lot of time to talk. He just said something like, 'There's a lot of history there.'"

There was a knock, but before we could even respond, the door opened and Layla came in. "Hey, guys," she said in a low voice. "I need to use your room for a second."

"What's going on?" Juliana asked.

She shut the door behind her. "I got this text—" She raised her hand, which had been pressed against her hip, and revealed the cell phone hidden in her palm. "I *have* to call my friend Campbell. Some guy she barely knows sent her this weird message, and she desperately needs to talk to me."

"You know you're not allowed to use cell phones in

the house," I said. "Call her back on the landline."

"I can't use the phone—Mom's downstairs and she'll hear."

"Jules and I are talking. Go call from your own room," I said.

"It's not fair that I have to share a room with Kaitlyn—she goes to sleep so friggin' early. And she's a tattletale. Just let me call Campbell, okay? I'll be fast." She looked back and forth between us. "You know who she is, right? Campbell McGill? Her dad is that guy on that show."

"That guy on that show?" I repeated.

"You know," she said. "On that entertainment news show—he's the whatchamacallit. The one who sits at the desk and says what the next story will be."

"The anchor?" Juliana said.

"Yes! That's it. Her dad's the anchor."

"I know who she means," Juliana said to me. "George McGill. He's on *Entertainment Access*, and Mom said he has a kid at Coral Tree. Not that it matters," she added, turning back to Layla. "You still can't use your cell phone in here."

"Just for like five minutes?"

"No," I said. "Now get out. We want to go to sleep."

She stamped her foot. "You guys are so mean. You get to have this room to yourselves and I'm stuck with stupid little Kaitlyn and her stupid little toys and her stupid little bedtime."

"I know it's hard to share a room with someone who's so much younger." Juliana stood up and tried to put her arm around Layla, but Layla knocked it away irritably. "I really am sorry. But it's best to stick to Mom and Dad's rules when we can. You know how they can be."

"I hate their rules," Layla said in a low, vicious voice. "I hate their rules and this family and everyone in it. It's the most repressive dictatorship anyone's ever had to live in and I'm going to run away first chance I get! God, I want *out* of here!" Clutching her cell phone against her chest, she flung herself out of our room and slammed the door behind her.

There was a pause.

Then Juliana said, "Well, at least she used some decent vocabulary words," and we both laughed.

"If we're really lucky, she won't talk to us for days," I said.

Jules moved over to her dresser and started to take off her earrings. "About all this other stuff, Lee-Lee, with Derek and Webster . . . promise me you'll reserve judgment until we know more."

"I'll try," I said. "If you'll promise me you won't automatically side with Derek because he's Chase's friend and Melinda Anton's son."

"I don't care who Derek's mother is," Juliana said

with an edge to her voice.

"Then you and I are the only two people in the world who don't." I slid off the bed and onto my feet. "I'm going to go brush my teeth." Out in the hallway, the light was on in the bathroom and the door was shut. As I approached, I heard the low murmur of a voice.

Layla had found a place to make her phone call after all.

I had less luck with my own phone call the next day. The home number listed in the school directory for Webster kept putting me through to a generic voice mail message, so I wasn't even sure it was the right one, and his cell phone wasn't listed. I really wanted to touch base with him about what had happened at the party, so I kept trying the useless home number.

"Are you calling Derek?" my mother asked, coming into the kitchen just as I'd put the phone down.

"Why would I be calling him?" I said irritably.

She just smiled coyly at me. And rather than embark on a useless attempt to introduce reality to my mother, I rolled my eyes and stormed up to my room—which was so much easier.

eight

Webster was already sitting in astronomy class when I got there on Monday. I nabbed the desk right next to him and said, "Give me your phone number, like, right now so I have it." Before he could even respond, I said, "I didn't blow you off on Saturday night—you know that, right?"

His blue eyes scanned my face uncertainly. "Really? I was told that you had made other plans for getting home."

"He said that? What a jerk."

"And, right on cue, he appears."

Derek Edwards had just entered the room and was being enthusiastically hailed by the usual sycophants. He glanced around and our eyes met. I instantly turned my shoulder to him and shifted closer to Webster. "I came out to find you, and you were already gone."

"What a mess." He shook his head. "I honestly

thought you were going home with your sister. You must have been so pissed off at me."

"Not even for a second. Derek told me he sent you away. I would have called you but—"

"Here." He ripped a corner off a piece of notebook paper and scribbled down his number. I did the same for him.

"I'm not allowed to use my cell in my house, though," I said, folding and pocketing the paper. "You can call the landline but be warned: my parents are pains in the butt if they answer."

"Isn't that why texting was invented?"

I shook my head. "Not allowed to do that at home, either. Sometimes we cheat when they're not looking— but if they caught us, we'd lose our phones altogether."

"Wow," he said. "They're strict."

"More weird than strict."

"Which makes them normal for parents." Then he said, a little sheepishly, "Elise, I thought you had ditched me. I mean, there aren't a lot of girls who wouldn't choose to go home with Derek Edwards over me."

"I wanted to go with you."

"I'm glad." He looked at me then—*really* looked at me. "You're different," he said softly.

I was pleased he could see that about me: that I didn't fall for status and fame like everyone else at that school.

He went on. "Anyway, the truth is, I was stupid

to go to that party in the first place. I knew better. It's just . . ." He hesitated, and right then Mr. Cantori looked up from whatever he was doing at his desk and said, "Why didn't someone tell me how late it was? Let's go over the homework. Elizabeth, read the first question."

Amid all the rustling of pages and Elizabeth's soft voice starting to read, Webster leaned over and whispered quickly, "I went to the party because I was hoping to see you there. And it was worth whatever happened because I did." Then he ducked down to get his book out of his backpack.

I just sat there, staring at the teacher without seeing him, feeling a smile play on my lips.

Juliana had to meet with her college counselor during lunch that day, so when I walked into the courtyard with my tray, I scanned the tables for someone else to sit with. I spotted Gifford but she was sitting with Chelsea, which amused me. Those girls defined the word *frenemies*: all Gifford ever wanted to do when we sat together in French and English (which we almost always did now) was complain about Chelsea, whose main appeal seemed to be the access she provided to handsome senior boys—and whose main drawback was that she didn't want to share said access with the devoted friend who couldn't stand her.

I looked around for another possibility, thinking maybe I'd just take my sandwich to a tree somewhere and read a book while I ate, when I heard someone calling my name. I turned and spotted Layla waving to me from the end of a nearby table. Another girl her age sat across from her.

"Hey," I said, coming over. "Aren't freshmen supposed to eat on the patio?"

Layla shrugged. "We felt like sneaking in here today. No one really cares."

"It's not that much fun, though," her friend said with a yawn. "It's kind of boring actually." She was a moonfaced girl with small blue eyes and expensively highlighted thick blond hair. She was a solid chunk from her broad shoulders to her square hips. Not fat. Just solid.

"You can sit with us if you want, Elise," Layla said, "but only if you promise to introduce us to some hot upperclassmen. That's why we're here. To meet guys."

"Ninth-grade boys are so lame," her friend said.

"The only difference between them and the seniors is a few years," I said. "And they'll outgrow that. What's your name?" I sat down next to her and across from Layla.

"Oh, that's Campbell," Layla said. "Campbell McGill." She caught my eye meaningfully, and I realized this was the girl whose father was on TV.

I sighed and wondered who the hell *didn't* have a famous parent at Coral Tree? Other than us.

Five minutes later, I was wistfully recalling my reading-under-a-tree plan and wishing I'd had the good sense to act on it.

Not that the conversation at our table wasn't riveting: Campbell complained that her sandwich had mustard instead of mayonnaise until Layla pointed out that it, in fact, had both. Layla spotted a cute guy and asked me if I knew him and I said I didn't and she called me a loser. Campbell cursed because she had managed to get mustard on the wrist of her Juicy Couture hoodie, and Layla wiped at it with a napkin. Layla pointed at another cute guy and asked me if I knew *him* and once again was disgusted that I didn't. Campbell asked Layla if she was going to eat all her chips, and Layla said she hadn't decided yet. Then she noticed another cute guy who she was sure I had to know because it wasn't possible for anyone to be so socially clueless . . . but it was possible and I didn't.

See what I mean? Riveting.

"This is useless," Layla said irritably. "You don't know anyone, Elise."

I was a little freaked by the hunger in Layla's eyes when each new guy appeared: she was so childish in so many ways, always arguing with Kaitlyn and trying to get extra dessert—no way was she mature enough to start dating. But girls her age did. I didn't at her age and neither did Juliana. But other girls did.

Campbell narrowed her eyes. "I thought you said she was good friends with Derek Edwards." Apparently, Campbell's own (admittedly minor) celebrity status didn't prevent her from getting excited about other people's.

"Really, Layla?" I glared at her. "Is that what you're going around telling people?"

"Well, it's true," she said defensively. "You guys have gone to parties together and stuff."

I was prevented from strangling my sister by the arrival of a very welcome Webster Grant at our table. "Elise! Fancy meeting you here. Of all the gin joints in all the towns in all the world . . ."

"Huh?" said Campbell McGill.

"It's from a movie." Webster transferred the Sprite he was holding to his left hand and offered her his right. "Hi! I'm a friend of Elise's."

I introduced them and she shook his hand with an excited look at Layla who bounced up in her seat. "Hi!" she said, snatching at Webster's hand as soon as he released Campbell's. "I'm Elise's sister Layla!"

"Of course you are," he said. "Everyone I meet is Elise's sister." We had run into Juliana in the hallway that morning, and I'd finally had a chance to officially introduce the two of them. Webster had been funny and charming, and she had given me a little nod that said, *Yeah, I get it.* He added, "How many of you Benton girls are there, anyway?"

"Four," I said. "But that's just a rough guesstimate."

"You all look alike, too. May I join you?" He swung his long, thin legs over the bench and settled in next to Layla.

"How come I've never seen you at lunch before?" I asked him.

"I usually skip it." He opened his soda. "I'd rather wait and eat something decent later. But I was grabbing a drink and saw you, so I figured I'd come say hi." He gulped at the can, tilting his head back so you could see his Adam's apple move up and down as he drank. Layla and Campbell watched him a little too intently.

On the plus side, the mood at the table had brightened a lot since a good-looking senior had joined us. Layla offered to go get him a brownie and he gave me a funny look but shrugged and said, "Sure," and Layla asked Campbell for money because she was out and Campbell obligingly pulled out her wallet and then Layla asked if Campbell wouldn't mind getting it herself so Campbell shrugged and got up and kind of slouched toward the cafeteria. I felt bad for her: so many of the girls at the school looked like they could be models and she looked . . . average. Not bad. Just average. Minus the designer clothing and expensive accessories, she'd fit in at almost any school in the country.

Just not *this* one.

"She was the girl you needed to reach on the phone this weekend, right?" I asked Layla when Campbell was out of hearing.

"Yeah," Layla said. "This idiot guy had sent her the rudest text." She lowered her voice. "I think Campbell thought he liked her so she was upset. But he's a total loser. *All* the guys in our class our losers—I wouldn't go out with any of them."

"Be careful about insulting freshman boys," Webster said. "I was once one myself, you know. And no girl would go out with me back then, which made for some long and painful nights."

"You've recovered nicely," I said.

"There are tears behind the painted smile, Elise."

Layla laughed a little too loudly. "Campbell's dad is the anchor for a TV show," she told Webster.

"Yeah, I know. George McGill, right?" Webster winked at me. "Seems a little more approachable than some of our other celebrity brats, don't you think?"

"It's a low bar." I had managed to avoid speaking to Derek since the excruciating drop-off at our house.

Campbell came trudging back toward us, her step heavy, her head low.

When she reached us, Layla grabbed the brownie out of her hand. "Thanks, Campby!" Campbell sat down next to me again, while Layla broke the brownie in two and gave half to Webster.

"That's all I get?" he said, popping it into his mouth.

"If you're good, you can have the rest." Layla waved the brownie at him with an archness I'd never seen in her before. She set it down on the table. "So are you guys going to the semiformal? It sucks that freshmen can't go unless they're invited by an upperclassman."

"It's a good rule," Webster said. "Keeps riffraff like you two out."

"Hey!" Layla slapped his arm lightly. "We resent that—right, Campby?"

"Yeah," Campbell said.

"So are you going?" Layla asked Webster.

"Don't know," he said. "Haven't thought about it yet." He snaked his hand out and snatched the remaining brownie. "I believe this is mine."

"I didn't say you could have it!" She made a grab for it, but he held it up in the air, on the side that was away from her, and even though she leaned over him trying to get it, she couldn't reach it. I leaned forward and neatly plucked it out of his hand.

"Hey!" he said. "Thief!"

"Give it back, Elise!" Layla crossed her arms, clearly annoyed that I'd ended their game. "It's his."

"It's mine now." I took a big bite.

"You're sneaky," Webster told me with an admiring grin.

"Teach you to wave chocolate in front of me."

nine

Juliana was back at lunch the next day and called me over when I came into the courtyard. Of course she was with Chase, and of course Derek joined us soon after.

Well, he joined the two of them, anyway—he and I barely acknowledged each other beyond a polite initial nod.

There was so much awkwardness between us now, after the party, and not just because of the Webster thing—I had promised Jules to try to reserve judgment about that, anyway.

The bigger problem was that Derek confused me. I mean, if I could have just stuck him in some "jerk friend of Juliana's boyfriend" category, I would have never given him another thought. But I was thrown by the brief glimpses of the charming Derek I'd seen while we were playing Ping-Pong together.

I honestly didn't know what to think about him, so it was easier just to avoid any direct interaction. Juliana and Chase were chatting away enough for all four of us, anyway.

It was funny how similar those two were. Like the way Chase laughed generously whenever anyone else made a joke, even a feeble one—that was exactly like Jules. He was basically the male version of her.

Which made me wonder: would I want to date the male version of myself?

Nah, I decided. Too boring. Let Chase and Jules share the same interests and eat the same foods and be lovable in the same ways and all that—*I* wanted someone who kept me on my toes, who made me question all my assumptions.

But he also had to be a good guy. That was non-negotiable.

It was a beautiful day, and after we'd eaten, Jules said she didn't feel like going back inside yet, so Chase led us around the building to a secluded little side yard I'd never seen before. We sat down under a tree and Juliana slipped off the sandals she was wearing and burrowed her bare toes into the grass with a noise of satisfaction. She had worn a summer dress that day—it was warm enough. Back in Massachusetts, we could only wear our summer dresses for maybe two months. But here they seemed to be good year-round.

"Hold on," Chase said suddenly. "I hear something." Then he jumped to his feet, grabbed Juliana's hand, and pulled her up. "Run!" he shouted. Derek and I scrambled after them as the sprinklers spurted and came to life.

We all made it off the grass just in time.

"Why would they go on now?" Juliana asked, as we watched the sprinkler heads whip around, sending powerful gusts of water high into the air. "Shouldn't they set them for later, when the students are gone?"

"I think they do it on purpose, to discourage us from sitting on the grass and ruining it," Chase said. "They only care about how it looks."

"Oh, no!" Juliana said with sudden realization. "My shoes!" She pointed back at the tree where the tops of her sandals peeked out above the grass.

"The sprinklers should go off eventually," Chase said.

"It's almost time for class." Juliana glanced down at her dress and sighed. "I'll just have to get wet."

"No, don't—I'll grab them," I said before Chase could. I knew he was about to offer, but I also knew that the leather shoes he was wearing were probably worth about ten times more than every item of clothing I had on put together, and I honestly didn't mind getting wet. "I'm wearing old jeans, anyway." I dashed across the lawn before either of them could argue.

Those were some mighty sprinklers they had at Coral Tree—top of the line, like everything else there. They shot the water so far and so high that I was drenched before I even got halfway to the tree.

I grabbed the sandals and ran back across. I handed Juliana her shoes. "They're soaked," I said.

"So are you," she pointed out.

"I know!" I said happily. I had forgotten how much fun it was to run through a sprinkler on a hot day. People walking by were staring at me, and I grinned back at them. "It's okay. I'll dry faster than your shoes will."

She slipped on the sandals. "Thanks, Lee-Lee. You're a good sister."

"I think I deserve a hug, don't you?" I advanced on her with my arms outstretched.

She screamed and shrank back. "Don't touch me!"

"You're hurting my feelings," I said. "And after all I've done for you." I turned to Chase. "Chase! How about you? Little love?" I went to embrace him and he backed off, laughing and saying, "No closer! No closer, *Lee-Lee*!"

"Oh, great, now you know my nickname," I said with a mock scowl. "*And* you rejected my hug. You really think it's so great to be dry? It takes talent to get wet on a sunny day, you know. I'm a maverick. I stand alone, wet and brave! You guys are just sheep."

"Exactly," Jules said, still cowering. "And wool should only be dry-cleaned. So stay away."

"*Baa,*" Chase agreed.

"How about you?" I asked, wheeling suddenly on Derek, who was standing nearby, watching us with that faint smile on his face. "Time to choose—are you a sheep or a maverick?"

"I'm going for innocent bystander," he said.

I shook my head. "Who among us is truly innocent?"

"How about a dry maverick then?"

"Not an option—but I think I could arrange a wet sheep type of deal for you." I let loose with a mad scientist laugh as I advanced on him.

He held his ground. "Do your worst, wet girl. I'm not afraid of a little water."

I stopped—I wasn't about to hug the guy for real— and threw up my arms in mock despair. "Well, then you don't make a very good sheep, do you?"

"Hold on," he said and leaned forward. He flicked at something on my cheek, his eyes briefly meeting mine as he did it. "Blade of grass," he said, shifting back. "Got it."

"How'd it get all the way up there?" I asked lightly, brushing at the spot with the back of my hand even though he'd said he got it.

"Some mysteries aren't meant to be solved."

I found myself grinning at him and then remembered that I didn't trust him.

Man, I hated not being able to figure someone out.

And from the slightly uncertain last look he gave me as we all parted to go to class, I suspected he felt the same way.

The next day, things got clearer for both of us.

I had gone to the library to do some homework during lunch and was heading back up the stairs that led toward my next class when I ran into Chase and Derek on their way down. Together, as usual.

Chase greeted me, saying they'd just dropped Juliana off at her locker. She'd had a test that morning, which she was worried she'd tanked. "So I gave her some chocolate and that seemed to calm her down," he said with a smile.

"M&M'S make the best pills," I agreed.

Awkward pause.

Then Chase kind of nudged Derek, who said abruptly, "Got a second, Elise?"

Chase immediately said, "Later!" and galloped down the rest of the stairs.

"Where are you headed?" Derek asked me. "I'll walk you to your next class."

"Won't that make you late for yours?"

"I have a free period." He turned and we moved up the stairs together, side by side.

I waited for him to say something else, but he was silent. I was curious about what he wanted from me—but was also determined not to help him out by speaking first.

A group of girls in volleyball uniforms passed us. "Hey, Derek!" one of them called out. He jerked his chin toward them in brief, uninterested acknowledgment.

We reached the top of the stairs and continued down the corridor in silence. We were getting close to my classroom. I said, "Well, this has been fun. We'll have to do it again sometime."

"Sorry. Hold on." He steered us over to the side of the corridor. "I was just getting up the courage."

"The courage?" I repeated. "To do what?"

Dark eyes flickered up to my face and then away again. "To ask you to go with me to the semiformal."

"Excuse me?" I had heard, actually, but the words didn't compute.

He cleared his throat and spoke a little more loudly. "I thought maybe you'd like to come with me to the semiformal."

"Me? Go with you?"

"Yeah." He looked at his hands. "Chase and Juliana thought it would be fun for us all to go together."

I was stunned. Part of me was like, *Holy shit, Derek Edwards just asked me to go to the semiformal with him!* But then I remembered I wasn't the kind of girl who cared about celebrity status.

On the other hand, I did like hanging out with him—or at least I did when he wasn't actively saying or doing something to make me despise him. Going with him might give me a chance to find out whether Derek was a good guy who sometimes acted like a jerk or a jerk who sometimes masqueraded as a good guy—something I was increasingly desperate to figure out. But if he *was* a jerk, did I really want to sentence myself to an entire evening with him?

He was going on. "If it's okay, maybe you and Juliana could meet us at Chase's house." He was assuming I'd say yes, which bugged me. "I think it would be easier if we didn't come pick you up this time, since your family can be a little—" He stopped and shrugged. "Well, you know. Better than I do, probably."

"A little what?" I asked warily.

"You know," he said again. "They make things difficult."

I backed into an Elise-sized opening between where the row of lockers ended and the stairway began. "I don't think so," I said.

He looked confused. "You don't think you know?"

131

"I don't think I want to go to the semiformal with you."

He took a step back. "Oh," he said. There was an uncomfortable pause. I noticed a piece of yellow fluff on the floor and wondered what it was from. Someone's sweater, maybe? It was a very bright yellow. You'd notice a sweater in that color.

Come to think of it, my mother had a sweater in that color.

Derek said, "You're not even going to give me an excuse? Like you need to wash your hair or something?" His lips curled like he was trying to smile, but it came off kind of weird and ugly, more like a grimace.

"Does it matter?"

"It's usually the polite thing to do."

"It's also usually polite not to say unpleasant things about people's families when you're asking them out."

"I'm sorry." He ran his fingers through his hair. A piece was left standing up awkwardly. "I figured you'd know what I meant. You seemed totally embarrassed by them the other night. So did Juliana." He was right: I had been and so had Jules. But they were still my family. "Forget I said that. I can pick you up at home if that's the problem."

"It doesn't matter," I said. "After what happened with Webster, I would have said no anyway."

His eyebrows drew together in a scowl. "You picked

sides on that one pretty quickly, didn't you?"

"Are you kidding? You threw him out of the party and then lied to him about my plans. It wasn't exactly a tough call."

"We had fun playing Ping-Pong. At least I thought we did. If other things hadn't—" He stopped. Then he said, "We get along when that guy isn't around. I thought if we went to the dance together, we could kind of start over again. Your sister thought so, too. She thought you'd want to go."

"Well, she was wrong." And it made me furious that Jules would speak for me.

He swung his head from side to side, eyes darting around like he was looking for the nearest exit. "This was a mistake."

"No argument here."

He recoiled. "I guess we're done, then."

"Right. Okay. Bye." I slipped out of my little hidey-hole and started to walk away.

"You didn't have to be so rude," he said from behind me, his voice strangely subdued. "I meant well."

I looked over my shoulder at him. "I'm sorry," I said. "But given the way you talked about my family and how you treated Webster the other night, I figured if I was rude, I was just speaking your language."

"You're quick to defend that guy," he said. "And to burn a lot of bridges while you're at it. You better make sure he deserves it."

"Don't worry about me."

"Worry about you?" He raised his chin. "I'm done even thinking about you." He turned and walked away.

"See you in astronomy," I said, in some feeble attempt to bring things back to a normal place. But he was already halfway down the stairs.

I avoided making eye contact with Derek later that day when I walked into class, and I wondered how long things would be this awkward between us. It wouldn't have mattered except for the whole Juliana and Chase situation—as long as they were a couple, we would have to at least be civil, but I wasn't sure either of us was capable of even that right then.

I felt miserable about how the conversation had gone: I hadn't intended for things to get so ugly, but he had totally insulted my mother and sister. They weren't *that* bad.

Well, maybe they were. But that didn't give him the right to say so.

Webster came a little late to class, and then we had to settle down for a pop quiz that was challenging only because Cantori had neglected to introduce most of the key concepts in it beforehand.

Webster and I gathered up our books at the end of class and walked out into the hallway. "So . . . I've been thinking, Cuz," he said. "Well, it's more of a question than a thought."

"What is it?"

"Would you go with me to the semiformal?"

"Oh, wow," I said. Then again: "Wow." I tried to think quickly. It would be fun to go with him—we'd laugh all night long—but it might make things weird with Juliana and Chase.

And was Derek going to ask someone else, and would they all go together with her then? Who would he ask? Chelsea? No danger of rejection with her.

"Elise?" Webster's light blue eyes were scanning my face uncertainly. "So what do you say? We could go to the dance then check out the after-party—"

I shook my head. "My mom's opposed to after-parties. We're not allowed to go to them."

"Even better," he said. "We can do something by ourselves. Unless you're going to break my heart and tell me you've already promised to go with someone else? Don't tell me that, Elise. Don't." I tried to respond, but he cut me off again before I could speak. "Don't. Please don't."

"I—"

"Don't!"

"But—"

"Don't, I beg you, don't."

I laughed and balanced my books in one arm, so I

could put my hand across his mouth. "Shut up! Or at least be quiet long enough for me to tell you I'm saying yes, I'd like to go with you. It sounds great." I removed my hand from his mouth. "Okay, now you can talk again."

"Well, now I can't," he said. "I'm speechless."

"You?" I raised my eyebrows. "Seems unlikely."

"How well you know me." His long, thin face lit up with a smile. "You make me happy, Miss Benton."

"I'm glad."

"Where are you headed?" he asked. "I'll walk you there. But I should warn you—it may be a little awkward walking next to me right now because, thanks to you, I'm walking on air."

"Is that faster or slower than walking on the floor?" I asked.

"It's just better."

"Well?" Juliana said, with an eager glance when we met by the minivan after school.

"Well what?" I slung my messenger bag off my shoulder and onto the ground, not meeting her eyes.

"Did Derek ask you?"

"To the semiformal? Yeah, he asked me."

She gave a silly little hop of excitement. "It'll be so much fun, Lee-Lee! We can go together!" She lowered her voice a little. "I know it sounds obnoxious, but so many girls would kill to go with him, so it's pretty nice that he wanted to ask you, don't you think? Not that I'm surprised. You're a million times smarter and prettier than any other girl around here." She stopped, finally registering my silence and the expression on my face. "Wait. What's wrong?"

I folded my arms. "You didn't actually think I'd say yes to him, did you?"

"You turned him down?"

I nodded.

"Why would you do that?"

"Do you really need to ask me that?"

"Because of Saturday night?" she said. "Because of the party and that guy—what's his name?"

"Webster." I hated the way she said "that guy," like he wasn't worth remembering. "And I've already made plans to go to the dance with him." I wondered if I should let her know what Derek had said about Mom and Layla. The problem was, knowing Juliana, she'd be all Gandhi-like and forgiving about his saying that ("Well, they were a little bit annoying that night, you have to admit"), and she'd make me question whether my anger was justified, even though of course it was. Jules was inhuman in her ability to forgive people. Better not to mention it. Instead I said, "Derek told me you said I'd be happy to go with him. Could you please not speak for me in the future?"

"Oh, Elise," she moaned. Like *I* had disappointed *her*.

"What?"

"Nothing. Let's just go home." She turned and opened the car door.

"Where's Layla?"

"She went over to her friend's house—the one with the weird name."

"Campbell McGill?" She gave a curt nod. I said, "I wonder about that friendship—" but Jules closed her door before I'd finished my sentence.

I went around to my side and got in.

"I don't know what your problem is," I said a few minutes later, when it became impossible to ignore the silent treatment she was giving me. "Two guys asked me to go out that night. I happen to like one and not the other. So what's the big deal?"

She twitched her shoulders irritably. "I thought you'd want to go with Derek."

"Why? Because his mother's Melinda Anton?"

"Why would you even say that to me?" she snapped. "Have I ever cared about stuff like that?"

"No," I said. "I'm sorry."

"You're so quick to assume the worst about everyone. Even me."

"Well, you were going on about how popular he was just a minute ago—"

"But that was only because I wanted you to feel good

about being asked. Not because *I* care." She bit her lip in silence for a moment and then burst out, "And now it's going to be so awkward at the dance. Chase can't stand Webster."

"For no reason except because Derek can't."

"Chase said Webster's a slimeball." She tightened her fingers around the steering wheel. "I'm sorry, Elise, but he did. I know you like the guy—"

"You'd like the guy, too, if you spent, like, three minutes talking to him. But you won't because your celebrity friends won't let you."

"That's just mean," she said. "And unfair. And untrue. And unworthy of you."

"Hey," I said. "You know what?"

"What?"

"Shut up."

And she did, but only after muttering, "You ruin everything."

ten

"I have to get another job," Juliana said later that night, as she poked through the pathetic remains of four years of babysitting and ice-cream-scooping money. She had apologized to me earlier that evening for being so angry about the semiformal, admitting I had a right to choose who I went with.

In turn, I apologized for telling her to shut up.

We never stayed mad at each other for long: we were too codependent.

"You could ask Mom to find out if anyone at school needs babysitting," I said.

"Yeah. But that's not going to help me right now." She was hoping to buy a new dress for the semiformal. Mom had told her they were more than happy to help— and had proudly handed her thirty dollars. Juliana and I both knew that most of the girls at school would be wearing Spanx that cost more than that. Which was why we were now huddled in our bedroom, staring at the small pile of bills. "Do you think Dad would let me get my allowance early, just this one time?"

"Go ahead and ask him," I said. "He loves giving that speech about how we're a nation of debtors and it all begins with kids borrowing from their parents. You'll make his day."

"Oh, what's the use?" She flicked at the money irritably. "I just wanted to look decent for once. Is that so wrong?"

"Dramatic much?" I got up and went over to my dresser and opened the wooden box on top. "You can get a decent dress at a thrift store for under a hundred bucks."

"I only have forty."

I came back to her bed and dropped the bills I had just taken out from the box onto her stomach. "Nope. You have sixty."

She sat up and grabbed the money. "Oh, Elise! Thank you! But don't you need it? You're going to the dance, too."

"It's not like I can buy anything with twenty dollars— might as well donate it to the cause."

"Okay, but we're sharing whatever I get."

"Both of us in one dress? We'll get looks."

"You're an idiot."

* * *

The next morning, Layla overheard us asking Mom if we could use her car (the answer was yes, but only if we did the supermarket shopping on the way home), and bugged us until we told her where we were going—and then bugged us until we agreed to let her come with us. As she literally danced around with delight, I felt a little guilty that Jules and I so often did things without including her.

But when she ran into the garage ahead of me and grabbed the front passenger seat with a triumphant "I call shotgun!" my goodwill toward her vanished.

"I'm older," I said, holding the door open and gesturing with my thumb. "Get in the back."

"But I got here first."

"We didn't have to let you come at all."

Juliana was climbing into the driver's seat. She said, "It's a ten-minute drive—not worth arguing over. Layla can sit in front on the way there, and you can have it on the way back, Elise." I grumbled but got in the back.

Once we were on our way, Layla kept punching at the radio—"Hate this song!" "Oh, this one's good—rats, it's ending," "Oh God, why won't Taylor Swift just *go away*?"—until even Juliana lost patience and snapped at her to stop changing stations.

The second we entered the thrift store, Layla said, "I need shoes," and ran off.

Juliana and I were wandering up and down the aisles

together when we ran into a couple of eleventh-grade girls I recognized from school. I was surprised: I didn't think Coral Tree girls shopped at thrift stores. They greeted me by name and seemed pleasantly surprised by the coincidence.

One of the girls—whose name, I kid you not, was Copper Fielding—had a great sense of style. I'd actually noticed her at school because of it. She was a master of high-low matching—a Gap tee with a Chloé skirt, say, or Levi's with a Chanel jacket. She was very tall, so everything looked great on her.

She asked what we were shopping for, and when I told her, she said, "I saw the perfect dress! It's too small for me, but it would fit you guys." We followed her to a rack of cocktail gowns, where she pulled out a dress. "It's a Dosa, from, like, three seasons ago. I can't believe it hasn't been snatched up already—they probably just put it out today. This would go for, like, two hundred dollars on eBay," she added. "I know because I sell stuff on eBay all the time."

The dress was beautiful in a shimmery rust-colored silk, but I instantly thought, *She'll have to wear something over it or Mom and Dad will never let her out of the house.* It was a bias-cut slip dress, very revealing, with spaghetti straps and a plunging neckline.

"Look," Copper said, and held the dress up against Juliana's body. "Nice, right?"

The color was beautiful against Juliana's dark hair and pale skin. "You have to get it," I said, as soon as she emerged from the fitting room to show me how it looked. "It's perfect."

She gestured to the bodice. "Mom and Dad—"

"I know. You'll wear a jacket over the dress at home and take it off when you leave."

Copper said, "You *have* to get it," and then she and her friends said they had to go check out the new merchandise at another thrift store—apparently shopping on the weekend was a regular sport for them, and they had a circuit to complete.

While Juliana changed, I went looking for Layla and found her over by the shoe rack.

"Hey, Lee-Lee. What do you think of these?" She held up a pair of red leather booties.

I wrinkled my nose. "They're way too beat up. Look—the heel's coming off that one."

She waved her hand dismissively. "I'll re-glue them. Most of the other shoes are in much worse shape. Can you lend me five dollars, though? I don't have enough."

"Maybe you just shouldn't get them."

"But I want them," she said, like that was all that mattered.

* * *

The night of the dance, Mom gave Juliana permission to wear as much makeup as she wanted, since she was a senior. "Just remember," she intoned, "less is more."

I wasn't given the same dispensation, so I had to confine myself to my usual touch of neutral blush and a strategic dusting of bronzer. Juliana—who looked *très* glamorous in her sparkling eye shadow and a smoky dark eyeliner—helped me fix my hair, pulling it up and back into a little pouf.

"You guys are so friggin' lucky," Layla moaned from my bed where she was stretched out, watching us get ready. "I wish I had a date tonight."

"Panty hose or not?" Juliana asked, holding up a pair.

"Are you crazy?" Layla said. "No one in Southern California wears them."

Jules hesitated. "Mom likes us to, though."

I shook my head. "Layla's right—and you know I don't say that lightly."

Juliana put the panty hose back in the drawer.

The dress fit her perfectly, and her curled hair fell beautifully over her bare shoulders. Then she slipped on a jacket and ruined the whole effect. She still looked moderately chic, just nowhere near as sexy.

"I hope I can take it off without Mom's noticing," she said, surveying her reflection with a sigh.

"It's too bad she'll be there," I said. "But the dress

looks cute either way. Really."

"Thanks. You look good, too."

"You think?" I looked down at my outfit dubiously—super-short dresses just weren't in anymore, not the way they'd been two years earlier when I'd bought it.

"I love turquoise on you," she said. "Makes your eyes look almost green."

"You're such a liar," I said, because my eyes were brown, with forays into hazelness on good days.

"Shh," Layla said. "Hear that? Phone!" She jumped to her feet, ran to the door, and flung it open just as Mom called my name. Layla halted. "Rats—it's for you, Elise."

The only two landline phones in the house were both corded because Dad had read an article about how electromagnetic rays in cordless phones fry your brain or something, so I had to go down to the kitchen to take the call.

Mom handed me the phone. "It's your date for the evening," she said stiffly. When I had first told her I was going to the dance a few days earlier, she had said delightedly, "With Derek, I presume?" When I said no, she didn't even try to hide her disappointment.

I was just grateful she didn't know that Derek had actually asked me and I'd turned him down—she never would have recovered from that horrific bit of news.

Come to think of it, I owed Juliana for not telling her about that.

"Hey," I said into the phone. "Hope you're not calling to tell me you're sick or anything."

I was joking, but Webster didn't laugh. "I am so sorry, Elise."

"Oh, no. What's going on?" I sank into a kitchen chair.

"I think I got food poisoning or something." He sounded awful, really wiped out. "I've been throwing up all afternoon. I hurled again, like, five minutes ago." He gave a weary hoarse laugh. "Sorry to be so explicit— I just wanted you to know that if there were any way I could still get myself there, I would. That's why I waited so long to call. But . . ."

"No worries," I said. "This stuff happens."

"Thanks for understanding. When I'm better, we'll make some other plans, okay?"

"Of course." We said good-bye and I hung up.

Mom was watching me like a hawk. She was already dressed for the evening in a crimson dress that she had paired—inexplicably—with yellow shoes. "What's going on?"

"He's sick."

"You can still go tonight," she said. "Most of the

kids won't have dates anyway. I'm sure you can find someone there to dance with."

I knew which "someone" she was hoping I'd find. "I'll think about it."

She looked at her watch. "I have to leave now."

"I can get a ride with Jules and Chase." I'd already decided I wasn't going, but if I said so, she'd try to change my mind.

"I'll expect to see you there." She picked up her green purse. (With a crimson dress and yellow shoes? Sometimes I wonder if my mother is simply color-blind.) "I'm off to the dance!"

Well, that made one of us.

I wandered back upstairs and told Juliana about the phone call.

"I'm sorry, Lee-Lee," she said with a consoling pat on my shoulder. "Come with me and Chase."

"It's too weird. If Derek's with Chase . . ." Actually, my real concern was if Derek was with someone else. A date. I'd look like a loser showing up alone after turning him down.

"Please, Lee-Lee? We'll have a good time, I promise. Please?" But this time Juliana's begging didn't work. I changed out of the dress and put my jeans and T-shirt back on.

Half an hour later, we heard Layla and Kaitlyn calling out, "The limo's here!"

Juliana moved toward the door. "I wish you were going with me," she said.

"Once you're with Chase, you won't even remember you have a sister," I said. "Have a great time, Jules."

She left the room, and I kneeled on the bed so I could look out the window. The limo driver and Chase had both gotten out of the car and were waiting for Juliana.

I couldn't see into the dark interior of the limo, and I wondered if Derek were inside and if he had found someone who'd said yes.

What was I thinking? Of course he had. He was Derek Edwards.

eleven

was still peering out the window when I heard Kaitlyn scream. Terrified, I raced out of the room and found her in my parents' bathroom, shrieking at the sight of blood dripping from her hand. There were bits of broken glass all over the place. Dad was downstairs in his office and must not have heard her cries.

I calmed her down, and she told me that she had accidentally knocked a glass jar of Mom's bath salts into the tub where it had shattered. Worried she'd get in trouble for breaking it, she had tried to clean it up herself and cut her finger on a shard of glass—not too badly, I discovered once I had helped her rinse it off, but it was bleeding enough to thoroughly freak her out.

Layla drifted in to see what the noise was all about

and idly informed us that the ancient Romans used to kill people by putting ground-up glass in their drinks, a fact that succeeded in eliciting new screams from her little sister who was now convinced she had inhaled glass powder and wouldn't survive the night.

I calmed her down from *that* and said to Layla, "I thought you were going over to Campbell's tonight." I pressed a fresh wad of cotton on Kaitlyn's wound.

"She canceled. Her dad has some big event he wanted her to go to."

"Oh. Well, I'm stuck home, too."

"Yeah, I heard."

"Want to watch a movie? We can check out what's available On Demand."

"Okay," she said. "I'll make popcorn." She stopped at the threshold. "But not a stupid PG movie. I'm old enough to see R ones now."

"But then I can't watch it," Kaitlyn wailed. "That's not fair."

"You can watch something for little kids in Mom and Dad's room," Layla said, with intentionally infuriating condescension as she left the room.

"I hate watching movies all by myself," Kaitlyn said.

"I'll stay with you. Hey, I think the bleeding's stopped." I lifted the bandage, and she looked down and saw the drying blood on it and started screaming all over again.

Oh, yeah, this was way more fun than any stupid old semiformal.

While Layla and Dad watched a movie that was, in fact, R-rated, to Layla's delight—and based on some literary novel, to Dad's—Kaitlyn and I curled up on the bed in my parents' room to watch some twee teenybopper romance that didn't have a chance in hell of distracting me from my thoughts.

I wondered if Juliana was having a good time.

Of course she was. She had gone to a dance with a guy she really liked. What was better than that? And she had looked beautiful tonight and they were probably dancing together right at this moment and then they'd ride back in his limo—

Would Derek be in the car with them? And if so, who else? I was tempted to sneak off and text Juliana to ask her if he had brought anyone to the dance, but then I thought Chase might see my text and think I cared who Derek had gone with, and I didn't care.

I mean, I was maybe a little curious. But I didn't *care*.

I got Kaitlyn to go to bed in time for me to join the others for the last few minutes of their movie and then lingered lazily on the sofa with Layla, watching one stupid TV show after another. Dad found us still in the same place over an hour later and wasn't happy.

"I'm especially disappointed in you, Elise," he said. "You usually use your time better."

"I'm tired," I said.

"So read a book. That's relaxing." Neither of us responded to that. He sighed. "I'm going to bed. Tell your mother to close up for the night when she gets back."

A little while later, we heard a car pull up in front of the house and Layla ran out. "Juliana's back!" she called from the hallway. I quickly scrambled off the sofa and out to the foyer where she was already heading out the open door. I hauled her back in and shoved it closed.

"What are you doing?" she said, twisting away from me. "I wanted to see the limo again."

"Juliana needs her privacy right now. When you're older, you'll understand."

"I understand now!" she said angrily. "Stop treating me like a baby, Elise. I get it. You think she wants to make out with him. God, you're a jerk!" She stormed angrily upstairs.

I stared after her for a moment, half laughing, half annoyed. She thought she got it, but she didn't really— that was the thing about Layla.

I heard Juliana's key in the door a moment later and opened it for her.

"Oh, good, it's you," she said wearily.

"Dad went to bed. Mom hasn't come home yet."

"I know. She was dealing with a situation." She shoved her fingers through her hair. "One that involved Chelsea Baldwin."

"What happened? What did I miss?"

"It's a long story."

"Tell me every detail."

She headed toward the stairs. "It begins with the fact that Chelsea was dateless."

I followed her. "Really? I thought she'd go with Derek."

Juliana shot me a look over her shoulder. "According to Chase, he only asked one girl, and when she said no, he decided not to go at all."

Why did I kind of feel relieved about that?

"Anyway, Chelsea kept saying she'd find someone to hang with there. So she splits off, which is great, but later she comes running over to me and Chase, and she's actually in tears—" She stopped abruptly as we reached the top of the stairs, because Layla was coming out of her room.

"What are you talking about?" she asked eagerly. "Who was in tears?"

"No one," Juliana said. "It's not important."

"Come on, tell me. You're telling Elise."

"Go to bed," I said. "It's late."

"Why do you guys always do this to me?" she said, her voice rising. "You always leave me out. I bet I know more about stuff like sex and parties than either of you!"

"I hope not," Jules said. "And keep your voice down—you'll wake up Dad and Kaitlyn."

"I hate you and your stupid secrets!" She slapped at my arm. "I know a secret you'd kill to find out, but just for that, I'm not going to tell you!" She turned on her heel and disappeared back into her room, slamming the door, which led—no surprise—to an audible complaint from her roommate.

"What was that about?" I asked Jules. "What secret would we kill to know?"

"She was just bluffing. Come on—let's talk in private." Juliana led me into our bedroom and shut the door.

I sat down on the edge of my bed. "Tell me what happened with Chelsea."

She pushed off her dress shoes, curled up against her pillows, and told me.

The story was this: Chelsea had slipped out of the hotel ballroom where the dance was being held to meet some random senior guy she'd been flirting with. One of the teachers happened to go out back to smoke and spied them sneaking sips from a flask and exchanging deep French kisses that had led to even more intimate fondling by the time my mother had been summoned and had arrived on the scene.

She confronted Chelsea and the senior, told them

that they would be suspended from school for three days and that she'd be calling their parents later that evening to notify them. Hence, Chelsea's tears. She clutched at Juliana as if they had always been BFFs. "You *have* to help me!" she sobbed. "You have to get your mother to back off!" And she had pulled Chase into it, too, begging him to help her persuade Juliana, "because otherwise I'll be grounded forever, you know I will! Dad will kill me, and then he'll ground me."

"He can't ground her if he's already killed her," I pointed out when Juliana quoted this to me. "Well, he can, but it wouldn't have the same impact."

Juliana wasn't amused. "Seriously, Elise, it was awful. Chelsea really expected me to go to work on Mom, and I think Chase kind of did, too."

"Mom wouldn't have changed her mind no matter what you said."

"I know. But . . ." Her attempt to explain this to Chelsea apparently hadn't gone over well. Chelsea accused her of being mean, of wanting to see her punished. "You never liked me!" Chelsea had spat out. "You think I get in your way with Chase! You probably told your mother to spy on me."

"Oh, now, that's logical," I said.

"I know, right? The drive home was so awful, Elise—Chelsea was angry and crying, and Chase was mad at her for being an idiot but also I think at me for not helping."

"He can't be mad about that. Chelsea got herself into this mess."

"Why does it have to be my mother who deals with it, though? I mean, I know why, but it sucks." Jules stood up and went over to the large green dresser that had belonged to Dad when he was a kid and had been repainted so many times you could see layers of colors wherever it was scratched.

"It'll blow over."

She didn't respond to that, just pulled a pair of violet pajamas out of a drawer. She started to get changed, so I figured our conversation was over and reached for the book I kept on my night table. I had read about a page of it when Juliana broke the silence. "He wanted me to go with him to the after-party."

I looked up. "Chase? Didn't you tell him we're not allowed?"

"Of course." She leaned against the dresser and retied her pajama bottoms. "So then he said it didn't have to be the after-party, we could just drop Chelsea off and go do something alone together later."

"You're here, so I'm guessing you said no."

"I'd already told Mom I was coming straight home."

"She'd probably understand if you said you were just

grabbing a bite or something."

"I guess. It seemed easier to come home." She hesitated, chewing on her lip for a moment, then came over and sat down on my bed. I curled up my legs to make more room for her. She said in a low voice, "I wasn't sure I wanted to go out."

"I thought you liked Chase."

"I do! More than I've ever liked a guy before. That's why I'm—" She stopped. "I feel stupid even saying this." She stared down at her hands. "I'm nervous, Elise. About being alone with him late at night. I've already done more with him than I've ever done with any guy."

"Really?" I closed my book and put it aside. "Like what?"

"Wow," she said with a laugh. "*That* got your attention."

"How far have you guys gone?"

"Not very. Chelsea went further with that guy tonight whose name she barely knows than I've gone with Chase." She hugged her knees up to her chest and rubbed her cheek against them. "It's not something I want to rush. But I'm getting the feeling that maybe he wants to be doing more, you know?"

"He's a guy," I said. "Of course he does. Does he push you?"

"Not in a bad way." She smiled a little private smile. "In nice ways, if you know what I mean. And he always stops when I tell him to stop. But then I worry that maybe I'm disappointing him." She rested her chin on her knees. "Anyway, it seemed like tonight could have gotten a little too intense, since he's leaving tomorrow. Plus the car ride was so—"

"Wait, he's going away tomorrow? Where?"

"There's some lacrosse showcase tournament. The boys' and girls' teams go together every year, and they stay in some hotel in San Francisco. It's not the actual season yet, so it's just for fun."

"Oh. Derek's on the team, too, right?"

"Yeah," she said. "He'll be gone, too. Why?"

"I was just thinking Chelsea should be pleased: she picked a good week to get suspended."

"I'll be sure to point that out to her, next time we talk." She sighed. "If there is a next time."

"There are worse things in life than getting the silent treatment from Chelsea Baldwin," I said. "Would you like me to start listing them? This could take a while. Let's see . . . rainbows, puppies, winning the lottery—" I would have gone on, except she threw a pillow in my face.

twelve

Webster was in astronomy class on Monday looking exhausted and thinner than ever—which I wouldn't have thought was possible. He kept apologizing for canceling. I told him not to worry, that it sounded like we hadn't missed much, except for a minor scandal.

"So that explains why Princess C isn't in class today," he said, when I told him about the suspension. "It's just not the same here without her. It's so strangely *pleasant*."

Poor Chelsea: no one mourned her. Earlier, in English, Gifford had gloated. "She always thinks she's above the rules. The old director used to let kids get away with anything if their parents were big donors like the Baldwins, so I think it's cool that your mother actually suspended her. She totally deserved it." She fingered the bejeweled elastic that held her perfectly smooth ponytail in place. "I'm going over to her house later today to keep her company—her parents totally grounded her for, like, the entire week. She needs her friends right now."

"It's good she's got you," I said, hiding a smile.

"Yeah, I know." She lowered her voice. "By the way, she is, like, so furious at your whole family right now—you know, because your mom suspended her and your sister didn't help and she said you've been really unpleasant to her from the beginning—"

"Wait, what did *I* do?"

The teacher called for our attention, and Gifford leaned over and whispered, "Don't worry about it, Elise. When she calms down, you can apologize. She'll get over it."

"Apologize for what?" I whispered back but she had already settled in her seat and didn't hear me.

That night, I came into our room and found Juliana sitting cross-legged on her bed, staring unhappily at her cell phone. I immediately shut the door behind me.

"What are you doing, Jules? If Mom and Dad catch you texting in the house—"

"Look at this, Elise. What do you think he means?"

She handed me the cell phone, and I peered at the screen. It was from Chase.

This is so much fun. Wish I never had to come back.

"It's a little weird, don't you think?" she said.

"He's probably just glad not to be doing homework."

"Still, he could have said he missed me." She smiled wanly. "Even if he didn't."

I had already staked out a couple of spaces at lunch the next day when Juliana rushed over. "Look at this one," she said, putting her tray down and handing me her phone. "And the one before it."

I scrolled through the messages: *too busy to talk* and *came here to get away—from evrythng!!!!*

"That's weird," I said.

"When we said good-bye, he was all like, 'I'll miss you so much—I'll text you whenever I can.' And now this." She sat down heavily on the bench with none of her usual grace. "I don't get it." She poked at her sandwich dispiritedly.

I kept staring at the texts, trying to make sense of them.

Suddenly I felt a hand on my shoulder. "No cell phone use during school hours. No exceptions."

"I'm sorry! I forgot." I dropped the phone on the table.

"You—and the phone—will have to come with me to the office so I can write up a warning slip. And you too, Juliana. You had an obligation to remind her of the rules and you didn't."

"Aren't the slips for our parents to sign?" I said. "Isn't it kind of pointless for you to give us one, Mom?"

"No exceptions," Mom repeated, and Juliana and I reluctantly got to our feet.

She marched us past all the other lunch tables. I saw about ten kids quickly hide cell phones on their laps as we moved through the courtyard, but there was no gain in pointing that out, so I stayed quiet and slouched sheepishly along at my mother's side like a naughty little toddler.

Juliana tried calling Chase that night from our home phone. She came up to our room after, upset. "I don't believe this—a girl answered his phone. She said he was too busy to talk and kept giggling. Elise—"

"Don't worry about it," I said. "Really, Jules. The girls' team went, too, right? They're probably all hanging out, and one of the girls just grabbed his phone to annoy him. I bet he calls you back in a second."

But he didn't. And it made me angry that he could leave her feeling anxious like that. *Come on, dude,* I thought. *Call her.*

I assumed that he and Derek were sharing a hotel room, and I told Jules that might explain what was going on. "The girls are all over Derek Edwards at school," I pointed out. "They're probably making up every excuse they can to stop by their room."

"That's not the most consoling thought," she said gloomily.

I dropped it but spent some time—when I should have been focusing on my homework—thinking about how Derek had said that stuff about Mom and Layla to me and wondering whether he had complained about them to Chase—and about me, too, since we hadn't exactly ended our last conversation on good terms. What if he decided he didn't want his best friend in the whole world—the guy who was like a brother to him—to have anything to do with Dr. Gardiner or her daughters?

And what if girls were crawling onto their hotel beds in skimpy lingerie, curling up with them to watch TV, and inviting them to romp in the hotel hot tub, giving Derek the perfect opportunity to maneuver Chase away from Juliana Benton and her annoying family?

I didn't say any of that to Juliana. I tried to keep anything I said to her about Chase upbeat and positive, but those thoughts bugged me and made *Richard III* even more incomprehensible than usual.

If I ever found out that Derek Edwards had said or done *anything* to make my sister unhappy, I would kill him.

First I'd kill him, then I'd ground him.

Chase did send a text later that evening, but only in answer to the one Juliana had quickly tapped out in our room while I guarded the door. Hers was: *Is everything okay?* His: *Im havng fun for the first time in weeks.*

What do you mean? she wrote back.

He answered a few minutes later. *My friends R right. UR a dead end.*

Juliana showed me the text. "I know what's happening now, Elise. He's fallen in love with some girl on the trip, and she's a lot more willing to do stuff than I am." She dropped the phone on her bed and curled up next to it in a fetal position.

"Maybe he's joking." I said, but I didn't believe it, and neither did Juliana.

"Yeah, because it's so funny."

"He likes you," I said. "Chase likes you."

She sat up and looked at me, eyes all swollen, cheeks red from rubbing against the mattress. "Apparently not."

I sank down onto my bed and lifted my arms, and then let them drop helplessly onto my lap. "I don't know, Jules. He seems so nice."

"Every guy seems nice until he's not." That was about the bleakest thing I'd ever heard Juliana say.

Layla had been sniping at me and Jules over every little thing, still angry that we'd refused to include her in our conversation after the semiformal. When she was snarky to Juliana out in the hallway a little while later, I couldn't take it anymore and told her so.

"Look," I said, "you can be as mad as you want at me, but go easy on Jules, will you? She's having a tough time right now."

"Why?"

"Doesn't matter. You should just—"

"See?" she said. "You don't trust me. So why should I even listen to you?"

I sighed. "If I tell you, will you promise to keep it to yourself?" She promised and I told her that it looked like maybe Chase was breaking up with Juliana.

"Oh, poor Jules," Layla said sincerely. She had a weird sort of loyalty to her sisters—it was one thing for her to make our lives miserable, but another thing entirely if someone else did. "He's an idiot. I'm glad you told me, Lee-Lee. I promise I'll be extra nice to Juliana." She was, too, bringing Jules a cup of tea, offering to give her a back rub—which Jules declined—and returning a necklace she had borrowed and "forgotten" to give back until then.

"What's going on with her?" Jules asked me when we were alone again. "Suddenly she can't be nice enough to me."

I confessed.

Juliana looked uneasy. "Make sure she knows not

to say anything to anyone, will you, Elise? If she goes around telling people that Chase broke up with me, it could be really embarrassing—it makes it sound like I thought we were more serious than he did, and I'll just look pathetic."

"I already told her to keep it quiet, but I'll tell her again." I found Layla vidchatting with Campbell. "Can I talk to you for a second?"

"BRB, Campy," she said to the computer and shut down the chat. She swiveled to face me. "What's up?"

I repeated Juliana's request and she said, "I *know*, Elise. I'm not going to tell anyone. Give me a little credit."

"Just wanted to make sure."

I stood up to go, but Layla said, "Hey, Elise?"

"What?"

"If you knew something—like, that someone had lied to me or Juliana—would you tell us even if you weren't supposed to?"

"What is this about?" I asked, sitting back down and eyeing her warily.

"Just answer the question. Would you?"

"If I thought you should have the information, then yeah. We're sisters. We have to look out for each other."

She nodded soberly and turned back toward the computer. "Hold on. I have to show you something."

She tapped on the keyboard. "Look." She tilted the screen toward me. I leaned forward so I could see it better: a photo of a man and a girl at a big dressy event. It looked like a father and daughter, although it was probably a mistake to jump to that conclusion, this being L.A. and all.

Then I recognized the girl. "That's your friend Campbell, right?" She was wearing a dress in a beige shade that wasn't particularly flattering to her dull skin, but her hair was arranged in a gorgeous (professionally styled) updo and she was wearing a ton of makeup. "Is that her father?"

"Yeah. Remember how I said she was going to some event with him last weekend?"

"Vaguely. He does look kind of familiar."

"He should. He's a TV star. And that's her mother, but you can't really see her." She pointed to a bare shoulder, an earring-ed lobe, and a beautifully curled lock of hair on George McGill's other side. "She's an actress, too. Campbell said she's on TV a lot, but just in small roles."

"Why are you showing me this?"

"Because of this." She pointed at whoever was sitting on Campbell's other side. He was slightly out of focus and would have been completely outside of the frame of the picture, except he was leaning in toward Campbell like he was about to say something to her, so a small amount of his profile had been caught by the camera. Something about the wavy hair and the skinny wrist poking out of his suit jacket seemed familiar.

I squinted at the computer. "Wait, is that *Webster*?"

"Yep. He went with Campbell and her parents to the awards show."

"I didn't know he knew her that well." I shrugged. "Weird. I'll have to ask him how he got invited along."

"That's not the point. This was Saturday night. *Saturday night*. The night Webster told you he couldn't go to the dance because he was sick."

"Oh." It sank in. "Is this the secret you were talking about, Lay? You knew that Webster lied to me so he could go with Campbell to this?"

She nodded. "I'm sorry, Lee-Lee. I would have told you sooner, only Campbell told me not to. She said Webster really wanted to go with her to this, but he didn't want to hurt your feelings."

"I'd rather have my feelings hurt than find out someone lied to me."

"Really?" That seemed to surprise her. She shrugged and went on. "Campbell thinks he's, like, totally in love with her. But there's no way. I mean, he's really cute. And she's—" Layla made a vague gesture in the direction of the computer screen. "She's my friend and all, but she's kind of . . . you know. Anyway, I think he just wanted to meet her dad and go to that thing—there were tons of celebrities there."

I nodded absently, distracted. I was trying to figure out how I felt about discovering that Webster Grant had blown me off so he could go to an awards show with a ninth grader and her showbiz father.

It was actually a little disturbing that I wasn't more outraged. Something about Webster made it easy for me to accept the idea that he'd lie to get out of an uncomfortable situation.

"Are you upset?" Layla was peering at me with concern.

"Nah," I said, and realized to my relief that it was true. "I'm fine."

My mother launched a stealth attack as I was heading back up the stairs—sprung out from where she was lurking, grabbed me by the arm, and hauled me into the empty living room. "What's going on with Juliana and Chase?" she demanded.

"What do you mean?"

"I asked her if they had plans for this weekend and she said she doubted it, and I got the feeling something was wrong." She shoved her glasses up her nose. "I didn't want to push her, of course."

Of course. Fine to tackle *me* in the hallway and try to get me to betray Juliana's confidence, but God forbid she ask the girl a simple question herself.

I tried to satisfy her curiosity without saying too much. "There's been some miscommunication, but I'm sure it'll all work out."

"Is it because I suspended his sister? She forced my hand, you know."

"I know, Mom. And so does Juliana. It's not your fault."

"First you and Derek, and now Juliana and Chase," she said, shaking her head. "Everything started off so well."

"Oh, please," I said. "There was never anything with me and Derek. He was only ever Chase's friend."

"Well, now he's not even that."

"Actually, I'm pretty sure they're still friends."

"Oh, you know what I mean," she snapped. She dropped my arm and turned away. "I need a glass of wine. See what you girls do to me?"

"I'm sorry?" I said feebly.

Back in our room, I asked Jules if she'd gotten any more texts, and she shook her head and said calmly, "I blocked his number." Then she changed the subject.

It was like she had cut off a fatally infected finger: it was painful, but she'd done what she needed to do.

thirteen

Webster greeted me with his usual enthusiasm in astronomy the next day and asked if we could make plans for the coming weekend. "If you're sad we didn't get to dance, we could go to a club. I'm the worst dancer you will ever meet in your life, but what I lack in rhythm and grace, I make up for with . . ." He stopped and shook his head. "Nope, I got nothing. But I'd make a fool of myself for you."

I said lightly, "Maybe you should check your schedule first. I'd hate for you to double-book again."

He cocked his head at me. "And by this she means . . . ?"

I cocked my head right back at him. "Does the name *George McGill* ring a bell?"

"Ah," he said with a long, drawn-out breath. "Busted." He held up his hands in a plea. "I'm so sorry, Elise. I'm a jerk and a coward. I should have just told you right away, but I—"

"Didn't want to hurt my feelings. I know."

He paused, and then he said, "Sounds like I made the wrong choice."

"Yeah, probably."

At the front of the classroom, Cantori called for everyone's attention.

"I'm an idiot," Webster whispered. "I should have told you the second Campbell invited me. But I felt so guilty. And I really *did* want to go to the dance with you, and was worried you'd think I didn't if I told you the truth. So it seemed more truthful to lie than to tell the truth, if you know what I mean."

"Not really."

"Let's talk more later."

I nodded, but class went late and I had to run to my next one.

I think we were both relieved not to have to continue the discussion anyway. I know I was. It wasn't like there was much to say. Webster had lied and we both knew it.

I wasn't all that hurt and I wasn't all that angry. It was more that when I looked at him now, his light blue eyes shifted away guiltily.

And that seriously damaged his charm for me.

The next morning, Gifford grabbed me in English class to inform me—with some glee—that Chelsea was back at school and "totally on the warpath" because of what my mom had done to her.

The lacrosse players also returned that day, in time for afternoon classes. I only realized it when Derek and Chelsea walked into astro together. I instantly wondered if Juliana had seen Chase and what had happened with that, but I'd have to wait to find out.

I was idly observing them from my seat when Chelsea noticed me. She whispered something in Derek's ear, and his eyes flickered coldly to my face as he nodded. He seemed angry at me, as angry as Chelsea. I had no idea if it was for her sake or his own, but it didn't really matter, since I was even more furious at him. I was pretty sure that he had something to do with the way Chase had treated Juliana, and if I ever got definite proof that he had a role in hurting my big sister—the one truly decent person in the world—his dislike for me would be nothing compared to my hatred for him.

Still, it's never pleasant being glared at. I looked away pretty quickly.

Webster was MIA for some reason, but given the way things had been between us lately, his absence was more of a relief than a disappointment.

I picked up a book and read until class started, at which point Cantori leaned roguishly against the SMART Board and told a jovial little anecdote about how he and "Mrs. Cantori" had gone for an evening walk, and she had been frustrated not to see any stars, and he'd had to explain that it was almost impossible to see them with the naked eye in a city like Los Angeles, where the lights and smog create a practically impenetrable mask.

"But with a telescope it's a different story," he said. "So, guys and gals, we're going to take a field trip! Next Friday, we'll set up some telescopes on the beach—"

"A field trip to the beach?" one of the girls said. "Oh my God. Where do we sign up?"

Cantori extended a cautionary hand. "Don't get too excited—it'll be dark out. No one's going swimming, and anyone who shows up in a bikini gets sent home. That goes double for you, Billy." Everyone laughed.

Billy pretended to be disappointed. "Aw, I was planning on wearing my itsy-bitsy teeny-weeny yellow polka-dot bikini!"

"Save it for the paparazzi," Cantori said, with a quick glance at Derek. "Anyway, I know this is late notice, guys, but it should be an amazing experience. The stars are aligned, both literally and figuratively. Does anyone have a conflict? Speak now or forever hold your peace." One girl raised her hand and said she had her SAT prep class that night. Cantori shook his head. "Skip it. I promise you this will be more educational in the long run."

"My parents will freak."

"Have a friend quiz you on vocabulary words on the bus." Cantori gestured to the desk behind him. "Everyone grab a bus form before you leave."

I ran into Juliana on the way to my next class. She looked awful. Her face was pale, and she had dark smudges under her eyes.

"Are you okay?" I asked, concerned.

She shook her head and pulled me over to the lockers, lowering her voice. "He's back and it's *awful*, Elise. I'm just trying to stay as far away as possible, but he keeps giving me these looks like he hates me now. And then I saw him laughing with this girl in history—I think she's probably the one I heard on the phone."

"Oh, Jules, I'm so sorry."

"I feel sick. I want to go home."

"You're just upset."

"I feel like I'm going to throw up."

"No one barfs from being sad."

Half an hour later, Juliana vomited three times in the girls' bathroom.

Mom officially excused me from my last class so I could drive Jules home. I dropped her off and was about to get back in the car to pick up Layla and Kaitlyn when I was hit by a sudden and intense wave of nausea. I barely made it to the downstairs powder room before losing my lunch.

Juliana and I spent the rest of the afternoon and most of the night taking turns throwing up in the hallway bathroom. At about two in the morning Kaitlyn joined us. It was oddly companionable: we were miserable but not lonely.

All three of us stayed home from school the next day. By early afternoon, Juliana and I were significantly better, and Kaitlyn had perked up by dinnertime.

"I never knew being heartsick was contagious," I said to Juliana.

"You were supposed to share my dress, not my virus," she replied with a weak smile.

"Stupid me. At least you got to come home like you wanted."

"I still have to go back next week and face him."

"You have the weekend to recover." We both knew I didn't mean from the stomach flu. "It'll be easier after that."

"I hope so," she said without the slightest trace of actual hope in her voice.

At lunch back in school on Monday, we sat alone far from our old table, and she said to me, "I think I'm okay now. It doesn't bother me to see him around. It's fine."

"Jules—"

"No, really, Lee-Lee." A pause. "The only thing that's weird is how angry he seems. I thought he'd feel bad, but instead he keeps glaring at me. Don't you think that's weird?"

"It's easier for people to feel angry than guilty," I said. "Maybe he's convinced himself he was justified in acting like an asshole—probably with a little help from Derek Edwards, who, by the way, keeps glaring at *me*."

"How could anyone be mad at you?" Juliana said loyally. "He must be as big a jerk as you always said. I'm sorry I didn't believe you right away. I should have."

"Yeah," I said, "you should have."

fourteen

As the week went on, the glares turned into pretending we didn't exist, which wasn't much better, but both Jules and I worked hard to return the favor, tossing our heads and laughing with other people as much as we could whenever we saw Chase and Derek.

Friday evening, Juliana dropped me back off at school for the field trip, and I found an empty seat on the bus next to a sophomore who had a big crush on Cantori. "He's the best teacher in the whole school," she said fervently. "He was my adviser last year, and he'd always take us out for french fries."

The Best Teacher in the Whole School unbuckled his seat belt soon after we left the parking lot, and wandered up and down the aisle, ignoring the annoyed glances the driver was throwing at him in the rearview mirror and chatting idly with the students like the host of a cocktail party, until we were almost at our destination.

Then he walked back up to the front of the bus, faced the rows of seats, and called for our attention. "Okay, so here's the plan. I was at the beach earlier today, where, with the help of a couple of friends who are still there waiting for us, I set up four telescopes, each of them focused on a different planet or star. I'm dividing you into four small groups." He fixed a couple of the gigglier girls with a look. "Let me repeat that so there's no confusion. *I* am dividing you into groups, and there will be no switching. You will stay with your group for the entire evening. You will take turns look-ing through the telescope, you will discuss what you see, and together you will sketch what you saw and describe it in scientific terms. This is a collaborative project—one finished packet per group." He eyed those girls again. "And I don't want to hear that you couldn't finish your work because one of your teammates wore plaid and you're wearing polka dots or because you like *him* and *he* likes someone else. Try to be grown-up about this, folks."

Billy Rodriguez raised his hand. "What if one of your team members is just really stupid or lazy? Can you kick them off the team?"

"Don't you worry, Billy," Cantori said jovially. "No one's kicking you off anything." Laughter from his fans. "Seriously, every person on this bus is capable of pulling his or her own weight, so just make it work, okay? To keep the teams as objective as possible—and, frankly, to make it easy on myself—I've grouped you by alphabetical order. Listen closely to your groups. Don't make me repeat them." He looked down at the clipboard in his hand. "Group One: Isaac Avenor. Chelsea Baldwin. Elise Benton. Derek Edwards. Sylvie Fine. Group Two: Webster Grant—"

"He's not here," someone called out.

"He's not?" Cantori turned to me. "Is he sick?" I realized he thought I'd know, since I sat with Webster in class.

I just shrugged, distracted. Why oh why did I have to get stuck with both Chelsea and Derek? Could my luck have been any worse? Isaac seemed like a hard worker, but Sylvie Fine was one of the Derek disciples. My only hope was that she and Chelsea would be so busy fighting for his attention that Isaac and I could just plow through the assignment and ignore the rest of them.

"Oh my God," said the girl sitting next to me. "You've got Derek Edwards in your group!"

"Yeah," I said. "Want to trade teams?"

"We're not allowed to," she said sadly.

As the bus rattled down a steep canyon road in the Palisades toward the ocean, I thought, *Hey, maybe the brakes won't work and the bus will crash and we'll all die.*

It was a nice thought, but we arrived safely at the beach a minute later.

We filed off the bus, and I said good-bye to my seatmate, who stopped to ask Cantori an unnecessary question. I trudged over to where the two girls on my team were already bookending Derek, and greeted them all. Sylvie said hi, but Chelsea gave Derek a raised-eyebrow look, and they pointedly ignored me. I felt my cheeks burn and looked out at the ocean like it was fascinating. Which I guess it was, being the ocean and all, but I was too uncomfortable at that moment to appreciate its wild beauty.

Isaac came off the bus a few moments later. He was a slight, small sophomore with overgrown curly brown hair, which he tugged on in moments of stress—which seemed to be most moments in his life.

He went straight for the packets Cantori was handing out and eagerly started leafing through the worksheets, while Cantori said, "You, my friends, will be at station number four." He pointed down the beach a little ways. "Your telescope is set up and pointing right at—" He stopped and shook his head with a grin. "Nope, I'm not going to tell you. I'll let you figure it out for yourselves. You have all the info you need to ID it in your packet."

Instead of his usual jacket and tie, he was wearing a T-shirt and Windbreaker, all very "cool guy in his off-hours" casual. His hair was ruffling a bit in the wind, and he gave me a wink that suggested he knew that every girl in the class had a crush on him, and he was okay with that.

I said to Isaac, "Let's go." We headed toward the telescope, the other three trailing behind us.

It was a beautiful evening, a little cool, but the breeze coming off the ocean was mild and left a salty taste on my lips. Back home—on the East Coast—an October wind could chill to the bone, but here it just gently moved my hair around. The sun had set, but the sky was pink and yellow above the horizon, and it wasn't completely dark out yet, just twilighty.

It was, I thought—a little wistfully—the perfect setting for a romantic evening. I wished I had someone to share it with.

As if on cue, Isaac spoke. His voice was low and soft. "Do you think he'll grade us as a team or as individuals?"

Guess our thoughts had been running in different directions.

I said I didn't know, and we arrived at the telescope that had a big "4" label dangling around its neck. "Let's see what we need to do first." Isaac started flipping through the pages of his packet. He glanced up at the sky anxiously. "It's getting too dark to read."

"Cantori said we should bring flashlights," Sylvie said. The three of them had caught up to us. "Did any of you guys bring one?"

Isaac yanked at his hair. "I never heard him say that. When did he say that? Was it in class? I never heard him say that."

"It was on the bus form."

"It looks like that group has two." I pointed to team three. "Maybe they'd lend us one." I looked at Derek. "They will if *you* ask." It was true, and since he already hated me, I figured I couldn't offend him any more.

"Fine," he said with a cold shrug. "I'll ask."

Sylvie immediately said, "I'll go with you," and attached herself to his side.

Outmaneuvered, Chelsea pouted angrily and looked around for someone to take it out on.

And there I was.

"Hey, Elise, how's your sister doing?" she asked with venomous sweetness. "I haven't seen her around much lately."

"She was sick."

"I see. And that explains why she and my brother aren't talking . . . how?"

"I don't know," I said. "Maybe he's a germophobe."

"Maybe he's realizing some people aren't as nice as they pretended to be at first."

"That's so true," I said. "Your brother *seemed* like such a good guy."

"Until your sister went all psycho on him."

"'Psycho'?" I repeated, genuinely surprised. "Juliana? What are you talking about?"

"We got it!" Sylvie sang out, waving the flashlight triumphantly as she and Derek rejoined us.

"She went totally psycho-bitch on him," Chelsea said, ignoring Sylvie. "Derek knows all about it, don't you, Derek?"

"I bet he does," I said.

"What's that supposed to mean?" Chelsea asked.

"All I know is that Chase spends a few days traveling alone with his buddy and suddenly he's like a different person."

"He's not the one who cut things off with no explanation," Derek growled.

"No," I agreed. "He's the one who sent nasty texts about how much fun he was having without her—and with someone else."

Chelsea said with an abrupt change of tone, "Come on, guys, we should get to work."

"I can read this now!" Isaac was shining the flashlight on the packet of information. "Who wants to use the telescope first? It's already aimed, so don't touch it except to focus."

"You go first," I said.

He scuttled over to the telescope and squinted into the eyepiece. "Cool! You guys have to see this! It's incredible."

No one moved. Derek was staring at me, his eyes narrowed to slits. "Wait—what do you mean 'nasty texts'?"

"One after another," I said. "Telling her how happy he was to be away from her."

"That's impossible," Derek said.

"I saw them myself."

Chelsea tugged on Derek's arm. "We only have, like, an hour to do all the work."

"I see it!" Isaac called out, still crouching but now waving a hand wildly. "I see . . . something. Wait, what is that?"

"Let me look," Sylvie said, and he obligingly ducked out of the way.

"You see it?" he asked, hovering. "You see it?"

"I don't see anything," she said. "Oh, wait—I think I'm closing the wrong eye."

"It's impossible," Derek said to me again. He irritably jerked his arm away from Chelsea's grip without even looking at her. "Chase didn't even have his phone."

"What are you talking about?"

"He didn't have his phone," he repeated impatiently. "People were sexting at the tourney last year, and the coaches from the different schools decided at the last minute just to ban all cell phones this time."

"But Juliana got a bunch of texts from Chase while you guys were gone."

"Why is this so hard for you to understand?" Then he said slowly and carefully, like I was a little kid, "He couldn't have sent any texts."

I thought for a moment. Then I looked over at Chelsea—who seemed suddenly fascinated by the pink clouds clustered at the horizon. My face got hot with anger. I turned back to Derek, whose own eyes were widening with sudden insight.

"Come here," he said, cutting off what I was about to say. He grabbed me by the wrist and pulled me down closer to the ocean, away from the others. Chelsea was watching and took a step to follow us, but Derek flashed her a savage *Stay away* look. She stopped but continued to watch us uneasily.

Derek didn't drop my arm until the sand was damp and packed under our feet. He faced me. "Okay. Let's go over what happened. Me first. Chase and I leave on this trip and all he'll talk about is how fantastic Juliana is. Then we get back and she refuses to talk to him or look at him—and she's blocked him from her phone. He has no idea why. Okay, your turn."

"Juliana was missing Chase like crazy, and then she started getting these super-nasty texts—sent from his phone—all about how he—"

He cut me off. "Chase didn't send any texts. End of story."

"Yeah, we've established that. But someone did." We both glanced up the beach at Chelsea, who pretended she wasn't watching us, even though she was.

Derek kicked at a piece of seaweed. "They were pretty bad, huh?"

I nodded. "He—or whoever it was—called her a 'dead end,' among other things. Then a girl answered his phone giggling, so she assumed he'd found someone else and was rubbing it in her face. She avoided him when he came home to make it easier on both of them. Juliana would never be mean."

"Neither would Chase." He groaned. "What a mess."

"We both know what happened, right? I mean, if Chase left his phone at home, and a girl answered it . . . it's pretty obvious."

"I can't believe she'd do that." We both looked up the sand again. Chelsea was wearing tight jeans and a sleeveless ruffled top that was too light for a fall night on the beach. She must have been freezing, but she looked great. Derek said, "She can be a total pain in the butt, but she and Chase are close, and this really hurt him."

"I can believe it," I said. "My mother had just suspended her from school, and she was mad at Juliana for not doing anything about it."

He considered that, his expression unreadable as he

watched Chelsea moving around the equipment.

"Also," I said, "people have a way of justifying what they're doing. I mean, if she looked at it as saving her brother from a really awful family . . ." I hesitated, and then said, "She wouldn't be the first person to feel that way about us, you know."

Flashlight beams shimmered in the dark around us like enormous drunken fireflies. "I have nothing against you or your sister," Derek said quietly. "And I'm sorry if I said anything offensive about your family."

"It's okay." I was surprised to find that I wasn't angry at him anymore. At least now I knew he hadn't poisoned Chase's mind against Juliana.

Someone else had done that.

We fell silent again. I kept sneaking little looks up at his face, though. And caught him sneaking one at mine.

Chelsea unwisely chose that moment to come fetch us. "You guys might want to think about helping out here," she said loftily, as she picked her way carefully through the sand. She was wearing platform sandals that I guess were better for the beach than her usual spike heels, but sneakers—like mine—would have made more sense. "I mean, *I* don't mind that you're not contributing, but the others might."

"Yeah, all right," Derek said tonelessly. He headed up the beach but said over his shoulder, "Sit with me on the bus, will you, Elise? I want to finish our conversation."

"Okay." I was following him back toward our group when Chelsea caught my arm.

"What did you say to him?" she hissed. "You said something about me, didn't you? He gave me a weird look. What did you say?"

"Maybe he's just not that into you," I suggested, and shrugged loose of her grip.

In the end, Derek, Isaac, and I did most of the work—or, more accurately, Isaac did most of it, and Derek and I helped. Chelsea sulked and Sylvie posed seductively against the telescope and occasionally wrote things down on the worksheets for us in her childishly round handwriting. Thanks to Isaac's nervous energy and focus, we finished up well before the allotted time, which left the five of us standing around with nothing to do.

Isaac offered to find some other planets with the telescope, and I told him I'd happily look at them. Sylvie and Chelsea were less entranced with the offer. Chelsea complained to Derek that she was freezing.

"Go wait on the bus," was Derek's uninterested response.

"Come with me?" You could see the nervousness in the look she gave him: she knew something was going on.

All he said was, "No, thanks."

Sylvie said, "I'm cold, too." Like Chelsea, she had

neglected to wear a jacket. "I'll go with you."

Chelsea waited one more moment, but Derek didn't show any signs of changing his mind, so she gave up, and the two girls moved off.

Derek and I stood side by side, watching Isaac fiddle with the telescope.

"So," Derek said.

"So," I agreed, and then we were silent again, but it felt amiable, like something had changed—yet again— between us. I didn't know if we were friends, but we weren't enemies, and that was an improvement over yesterday. Which made me wonder what tomorrow would bring.

Given our history, probably more enmity. We never seemed to be able to stay friends for long. At this moment, now that I wasn't actively angry at him, that seemed kind of sad to me.

People were goofing off all around us. It was nighttime, we were on the beach, and the weekend was beckoning. A couple of guys had rolled up their pants and waded into the water.

"You tempted?" Derek asked lightly, gesturing toward them. "I know how much you like to get wet."

"Only when I'm unique. Other wet people cheapen the experience."

Cantori came racing down to the ocean, yelling at the waders to get out immediately. "Cut it out! This is a liability issue for the school!" No trace of his usual geniality. Guess he was having a rough night.

"So much for that idea," Derek said as the boys cheerfully complied.

"I can't find anything." Isaac twisted around to look at us. "I think something's wrong with the telescope."

"Don't worry about it," I said. "It's such a beautiful night. Just enjoy it."

Isaac wasn't the kind of kid to stand around gazing up at the stars—he was the kind of kid to stoop, peering into a telescope at the stars. So he went back to doing that.

The moon had moved higher in the sky, and it was actually easier to see now than it had been earlier. I stole another peek at Derek.

I had disliked him so much before, and all that not liking him had been a sort of defense against his handsomeness. Whenever I used to look at his face, I'd convince myself that all I saw were the proud, pampered looks of a celebrity brat. But now that I wasn't hating him so much—hardly hating him at all, really—I mean, almost not at all—I was suddenly aware of how his cheekbones slanted under his dark and thoughtful eyes.

It made me think that maybe I should have gone to the semiformal with him.

* * *

Cantori must have suddenly noticed the change in mood from scholarly to celebratory—half the class was now working on an enormous sand castle—because he abruptly called for our attention and told us all to get back on the bus. He stayed behind with his friends to help pack up the telescopes and wearily waved us on our way.

Derek scored us an empty bench and let me slide in first, so I could have the window seat. We put on our seat belts and listened to the bus driver's obligatory safety speech about exit windows and what to do in an emergency.

And then . . . silence.

Awkward silence.

Really awkward silence.

All around us, people were chattering away, laughing, gossiping, screaming, whispering . . .

And we continued to say nothing while the bus rolled out of the big parking lot and onto the Pacific Coast Highway. I actually thought we'd make it the entire twenty minutes to school without either of us saying a word, and was wondering why Derek had even bothered to sit with me when he finally spoke.

"We have to get them back together."

By the time the bus parked in front of the school, we had what you might call a plan.

Derek took hold of the seat in front of us and swung himself up into the aisle. He held out his hand toward me. I took it and started to rise smoothly to my feet—

Only to be slammed back at the waist by the seat belt I'd forgotten to undo.

"Fail," I said, ducking my head to cover my embarrassment as I let go of his hand and quickly unfastened the buckle.

"At least you were safe at any speed." He grinned down at me, his hand still extended.

Derek Edwards was smiling at me again, after a week and a half of glares.

It didn't suck.

I took his hand once more, and this time managed to get up without any additional humiliation. As I slid into the aisle, the guy behind me—a junior named Jesse—tapped me on the shoulder. "Hey," he said. "Webster never showed and he was supposed to be on my team. You know what the story is?"

I quickly said, "No idea," but his question had wiped the smile off Derek's face.

He dropped my hand and faced front.

I didn't know much about Jesse, but he sure had lousy timing.

FiFteen

I had called home as we were packing up to leave the beach, so Juliana was already waiting at school for me in the minivan. As soon as I opened the car door, she said, "We have to hurry. Mom's a wreck and Dad asked me to come back as quickly as possible."

"What's wrong with Mom?" I asked, getting in.

"The parents of that boy she suspended—the one who was making out with Chelsea—called the head of the Board of Trustees to complain about her."

"You're kidding!"

She shook her head as she pulled out of the lot. "She was on the phone for two hours defending herself—like *she* had done something wrong, not them."

"That's so unfair."

"I know. Her job's tough."

"We should be more supportive."

"We really should."

"On another matter . . ." I told her about Chase's cell phone.

Like I had earlier, she took a while to absorb the information. "He definitely didn't have it with him?"

"Definitely. Come on, Jules, think about it. It's totally not like Chase to say those things."

"But I've spent the last few days convincing myself it is." She thought some more. "You really think it was Chelsea?"

"He left his phone at home. Who else?"

"Why would she do that? I thought we got along okay. Except for that night when—" She halted. "That's why. Because I didn't help her with Mom."

"You have my permission to loathe her."

"So he really didn't write those things! I should—" She gasped suddenly. "Oh my God, Elise!"

"What?"

"I've been such a jerk to him since he came back!"

"Don't worry," I said. "Derek promised me he'd explain the whole thing to Chase. He was sure he would understand."

"I hope so. I'll apologize a million times over."

"Just give Derek time to explain first. It will be easier."

She nodded. There was a brief pause. She said slowly, "So you and Derek worked this whole thing out together?"

"Yeah." I tried to sound casual about it. "It was

funny because at first we were both so angry and defensive, but then once we realized what had happened, all he could say was how much Chase adores you."

"That was *all* he could say?" she asked, a little coyly. "Are you sure?"

"What else did you want?"

"I don't know," she said, "but you keep smiling like you're not telling me everything."

"I'm telling you everything," I said. Smiling.

Our resolve to be more supportive of Mom was put to the test as soon as we got home. In between sips of wine, she recounted every sentence of her two-hour-long reaming-out by phone that afternoon. I felt sorry for her. I also desperately wanted to escape and be alone with my thoughts. There was a lot I needed to think about.

Juliana was pouring Mom a refill when we all heard Layla call out, "Doorbell! I got it!" Then, a moment later, "Jules! Come quick!"

Juliana and I both ran into the foyer just as Layla opened the door to Chelsea Baldwin.

Really? Chelsea?

It made more sense when I realized that Chase was right behind her, his hand firmly on her shoulder, holding her in place.

He wasn't looking at me, though. Or at Layla, who

stood in the open doorway. Or at Mom, who had come up behind the rest of us.

No, Chase had eyes for only one person—and she was staring back at him in openmouthed surprise.

"My sister needs to tell you something," he said.

"Not in front of the whole family," Chelsea snapped.

"I'll come out." Juliana's fingers reached out blindly and caught mine. "Come with me."

"Can I come, too?" Layla asked.

"No," we said in unison, as the two Baldwin siblings stepped back to let us out and I closed the door behind us.

Derek's car was parked in front of our house, its driver still in the front seat. Our eyes met through the window. He reached for the door handle and got out.

Meanwhile, Chelsea was saying to Jules in a flat robotic monotone, "I'm sorry for any confusion I might have caused. I was fooling around with Chase's phone this week, and I might have accidentally sent you some joke texts." She scowled at her brother and said in her normal voice, "There, are you happy?"

"Not with you."

"It was just a joke. You guys need to grow a sense of humor."

"It wasn't funny," Chase said. "It was mean."

"Yeah? Well, her mother suspended me and she didn't even lift a finger to—"

He whipped around. "Shut up and go wait in the car!" I didn't know the guy had it in him to sound that fierce—nice to know he could be tough when he needed to.

Chelsea quickly backed away.

Derek was leaning against his car, arms folded, watching us. As she reached him, Chelsea stopped and said something, but he just shook his head without even looking at her. She threw herself into the backseat of his car and slammed the door.

Juliana released my hand, which was a relief since she had been gripping it too tightly, and stepped toward Chase. "I am so sorry," she said hoarsely. "You must have thought I was just being horrible to you."

"I was definitely confused." He touched her arm lightly with his index finger. "But now that we both know what happened—"

As they moved closer together, I slipped quietly away and walked down to where Derek was waiting. He stood upright as I approached.

"Thank you," I said.

"I didn't do anything except tell Chase what happened."

"You got him here."

I noticed Chelsea glaring at us through the car window. Derek followed my gaze, and Chelsea raised her arm to tap her watch meaningfully with her index finger. I said to Derek, "I didn't think Chase ever got angry, but just now he sounded like he was ready to kill her."

"I had to drag him away from her when he first found out—his hands were going for her throat."

"Yeah? Why'd you stop him?"

"Not for her sake, trust me. I just didn't want him to end up in jail."

"You could have let him choke her a *little* bit," I said. "Just enough so she couldn't, you know . . . swallow a Jamba Juice for a week, say."

"No smoothies for a whole week?" He shook his head. "Death would be kinder."

"Life without—" I stopped because the front door opened and my mother emerged.

"Why don't you boys come inside?" she called out. "I'll put out some milk and cookies." Her words were slightly slurred. Just slightly. Enough for me to know she'd made short work of that second (third?) glass of wine Juliana had poured for her. Enough for me to desperately not want the boys to come into our home.

Fortunately, Chase said, "Thanks, Dr. Gardiner, but I need to get my sister back." He turned to Juliana. "I just wanted to ask you . . . There's a premiere tomorrow night for Derek's mother's new movie. Can you come with us?"

Before Jules could answer, Layla suddenly pushed

past my mother and came racing down the front walk. "Can I come, too?" she asked excitedly. "I've always wanted to go to a movie premiere!"

"Layla!" I said angrily.

"I'm just asking—they can say no. God, Elise, you act like you're in charge of everything."

"*I'm* saying no."

"No for your sister or no for you?" Derek asked uncertainly.

"Me?" I took a surprised step back. "Am I invited?"

He toed a clod of grass with the tip of his sneaker. "Yeah. You and Juliana like doing stuff together, right? And it's no problem getting another ticket."

I wanted to go, but not if he didn't really want me to. "If you're worried that Juliana won't go without me, we're not really that codependent. You don't—"

He cut me off. "It's not just that." Quick glance up at me and then the clod of grass regained his interest. He kicked at it lightly. "I think it would be fun. Give me someone to talk to while Chase and Juliana are . . . you know."

"Yeah—they can get distracted when they're together."

"Exactly. So will you come keep me company?"

"Yes, I'd like that," I said. Since he put it that way . . . "Thanks."

Derek and I moved up toward Juliana and Chase,

and he told them that I was coming, too. Jules squealed and bounced happily on the balls of her feet.

"Great! We'll pick you both up tomorrow around seven," Chase said. "Come on, D, let's hit the road."

They had driven off, and Jules and I were heading back toward the house when Layla blocked our way. "I hate you both," she said, stamping her dirty bare foot. "Especially you, Elise! He probably would have let me come if you hadn't told him not to. You leave me out of everything. I hate this whole stupid family!" She ran past us and into the house, slamming the door behind her.

"Wow," I said. "Even for her, that was over the top."

"Oh, who cares!" Juliana exclaimed with sudden, surprising gaiety. She twirled around. "He still likes me, Elise!"

"We were both idiots to think he could have stopped. But will you finally now admit that Chelsea is the devil's spawn?"

"Rosemary's baby," she agreed.

We headed up the path. "We have to find a way to make her pay for this," I said.

Juliana opened the front door and held it for me. "You already have."

"What do you mean?"

"By going to this thing tomorrow night with Derek."

"He only invited me because of you and Chase."

"Right," she said, following me inside. "He's never shown the slightest interest in you before. I mean, he's never stared at you like you're the only person in the room when we're all together. Or sulked around for days because you turned him down for a dance. Or touched the sleeve of your sweater when he thinks no one's looking—"

"He's never done any of that," I said. Then, less confidently, "Has he?"

She laughed. "You know, you're right. He's obviously only inviting you for my sake. It's all for my sake. That's the only reason. It's—"

"Oh, just shut up," I said. I was too confused about my own feelings to be teased about someone else's.

sixteen

That night, I was clicking back and forth between my English paper and an online chat with a couple of friends from Amherst who should have been asleep, given the time difference, but one of them was excited about a guy and one was in despair about a guy, so they were both up. I was just on the verge of telling them I really had to get some work done when I noticed I had an email from an address I'd never seen before and clicked on that instead.

It was very long. I scrolled down and read the name: Derek.

That was unexpected. And oddly unsettling. I eagerly returned to the top.

My eagerness wasn't at all diminished as I read: every word fed it until I was reading as fast as I could, my eyes sweeping the screen as I tapped the scroll bar faster and faster.

Hi, Elise.

I've been trying to decide if I should write or not and finally decided I should. I figured why not clear the air before tomorrow night. A fresh start and all that.

First of all, I want to apologize. I've thought back to what I said about your family when I asked you to the semiformal and realized how rude it was. I'm sorry. No wonder you didn't want to go with me.

More importantly—and more awkwardly—I feel like I should tell you a little more about what happened with my family and Webster Grant.

I know I can trust you not to repeat any of this.

He told you we were friends and I guess we were. Friendly anyway. He was always just sort of THERE, and he was fairly entertaining, so I didn't mind.

But when he started coming over to my house, things got weird pretty fast. He kept trying to wrangle his way into my parents' company. And then I found him looking through the drawers in their bedroom when he was supposedly going to the bathroom. I didn't say anything about it—I just didn't invite him over again. He was creeping me out.

Georgia really liked him—he always spent time talking to her—and I guess once it was clear I wasn't going to be his ticket to my parents, he went after her instead. One day she told me they were "going out."

My parents and I went ballistic—on top of everything else, she's like four years younger than he is. They wouldn't let her date him. She insisted they were in love. We all figured he'd lose interest pretty quickly since he could only see her at school. And he did. Only he figured he'd get something out of it first. So he got her to sneak out and meet him one night, got her drunk— she'd never had more than a sip of wine before—and took some embarrassing photos of her. He didn't even have the decency to take her home, just left her at a mall all alone after dark. She wandered around for a while, trashed and confused. Fortunately, a security guard got concerned and used her cell phone to call us.

A couple of the photos appeared on some online gossip site, but my parents' PR people got them killed pretty quickly.

Georgia was already shy and nervous. This put her over the edge. She couldn't face going back to school, just broke down when she tried. The school she's in now is for girls with emotional issues. It's been good for her. She feels safe there.

I know you consider the guy a friend. But every time I look at him, I think about how he messed up Georgia's life. If it weren't for him, she'd still be living at home, going to Coral Tree.

So that's the story. We don't have to talk about this at the premiere—in fact, I'd prefer not to talk about it ever—but I really wanted you to know. No one can confirm it for you because I've never told anyone else, so I guess it's up to you whether you believe it or not.

Derek

"My God."
I realized I had spoken out loud and was relieved that

Jules was already asleep. Otherwise, she'd have asked what I was talking about and I couldn't tell her. Derek was trusting me to keep it confidential and I would.

I believed him. No question about that.

Webster had lied to me to go out with Campbell because of who her father was. Everything Derek said fit with that. Webster's charm and my stupid determination to show what an egalitarian I was by siding against the guy I had already decided was a total celebrity brat had succeeded in convincing me that Webster was some kind of victim and Derek some kind of aggressor.

I had picked the wrong side from the start.

I hit reply and sat there trying out various responses for a while before I finally settled on one.

> I believe you. Thanks for telling me. I'm so sorry for your sister. I'll see you tomorrow night.
>
> Elise
>
> P.S. Webster isn't my friend anymore, anyway.

I sent it but didn't return to chatting with my friends. I tried to work but kept obsessively checking my email to see if Derek had replied to my reply until I finally closed my laptop an hour or so later and went to bed.

But I couldn't sleep. I felt awful that I hadn't believed Derek about Webster in the first place, had acted all high and mighty—Elise Benton wasn't about to fall all over someone just because his parents were famous. Oh, no. I was way too smart, way too intuitive, way too perceptive to do *that*.

I was an idiot.

And Webster was a horrible human being.

And Derek was . . . what?

A pair of dark eyes that hid more than they revealed and some broad shoulders and a mouth that could be cold and thin and then suddenly widen into a generous grin just when you thought such a thing was impossible.

Maybe he was my friend now, too?

I hoped so but wasn't sure I deserved his friendship. I had misunderstood and misjudged him from the beginning.

I flipped onto my other side.

On top of everything else, I shouldn't have been so mean to him when he invited me to the dance. He was right: Layla always managed to embarrass me, and Mom, too. He was only being honest about that.

I turned onto my back. I could hear Juliana's soft and steady sleeping breaths. She, at least, was fine with the state of things tonight. She wasn't tortured by what she should and shouldn't have said in the past, by how stupid and prejudiced she'd been when she should have been smart and open-minded.

Nope. That was me.

At some point early in the morning I fell asleep, but as soon as I woke up, I checked my email. Still nothing from Derek. Was he angry? Should I have said more in my response?

I wiggled my fingers over the keyboard uncertainly. Should I write something else?

No, that would look needy.

Anyway, what more did I want from him? He had told me something he hadn't told anyone else. He wouldn't have trusted someone he hated with a secret, right?

I hugged that thought to me all day as I did some homework and then joined Juliana in primping for the movie premiere.

We were slipping on our shoes when Chase and Derek pulled up in front of the house at exactly seven the following night—in Chase's car, not the limo, which was a relief.

By the time we made it downstairs, Dad had already opened the front door and Chase and Derek were waiting for us inside the foyer. Mom was out at a school function of some sort, so at least it was only Dad greeting them—but he could be embarrassing in his own way.

Juliana ran down faster than I did. Chase met her at the bottom of the staircase where he took her hand and gave her a very quick, chaste kiss on the cheek. Dad nodded his approval.

At first I was concentrating on picking my way

carefully down the stairs in my high heels, but as I got near the bottom, I looked up and saw that Derek was wearing a sports coat over a white shirt, no tie, the buttons open at his throat. His neck was strong, his chin tilted up as he watched me, his mouth parted just enough to show a glint of straight white teeth—

I realized I was totally staring at him—and Dad and Juliana and Chase and Kaitlyn were all right there. I broke my gaze, swallowed hard, and said, "Am I okay?" in a voice that came out awkwardly squeaky. I was wearing the rust-colored slip dress that Juliana had worn to the dance (with the same jacket over it until I got out of the house).

"Yeah," Derek said. "You're okay."

You know, he was a man of few words, but each one felt like it carried a lot of weight.

Chase said, "You look amazing, Elise. You both look amazing."

"What about me?" asked a voice from above, and Layla came skittering down the stairs. She was wearing tight blue jeans and a gauzy shirt with a gathered top that I suspected could be pulled down off the shoulder, but which at the moment was demurely pulled up to create a wide neckline. Her hair was curled, and she was wearing a ton of eye shadow and lip gloss. "How do *I* look?"

"Go wash your face," Dad barked. "You're too young to be wearing all that gunk on it."

"Oh, Daddy, it's just tinted moisturizer," she said blithely. "It'll all be absorbed in a minute."

His brow furrowed uncertainly. He was suspicious but also aware of his own ignorance in these matters. He satisfied himself with a brusque "I'll be the judge of that."

"No time," she said. "I'm meeting Campbell at Starbucks. Can you give me a lift?" she asked Chase. "It's only like three blocks away."

We divided up into boys in the front seat, girls in the back.

"So what are your plans for tonight?" I asked Layla.

"Just hanging out."

"You're awfully dressed up for Starbucks."

"So? I wanted to look nice."

When we dropped her off, I watched her walk into the dark-windowed coffee shop, clutching a panda bear purse and wobbling in heels that were too high for her.

A half hour later, Chase parked his car in a huge garage in Hollywood and we all got out. I shed my jacket, and Chase locked it in the trunk for me. "You sure you won't be cold?" he asked me.

"Probably. But—"

"What price beauty?"

"Exactly."

"Now we walk." Chase took Juliana's arm and led

the way to the stairs out of the parking garage and onto Hollywood Boulevard.

Derek and I fell back a few paces behind them. The night was cool, and I wasn't wearing much other than that thin slip, but I was shivering with excitement, not cold.

I glanced sideways at him. I didn't feel like I should bring up the email since he hadn't mentioned it. But it was weird not bringing it up. His face was impassive, impossible to read. And I didn't even know how to begin. "Thanks for telling me all that horrible stuff that happened to your sister"?

Better to wait and let him bring it up. If he did.

You could see the movie theater we were going to from a block away: there were huge searchlights, and the whole area was cordoned off with police officers and security guards patrolling the edges. People were thronged outside the velvet ropes: tourists, who had probably just come to Grauman's Chinese Theatre to see its famous footprints and then discovered with delight that an actual movie premiere was going on, with Melinda Anton herself in attendance.

"Wow," I said. "The whole red-carpet thing is for real."

"Yeah," Derek said heavily. "It's real."

"I'm sorry. I'll probably say lots of stupid things tonight. Do you mind?"

"No." Like I said: a man of few words.

"Do you like going to these things? It must be cool seeing your parents up on the screen." He didn't reply immediately, so I added sheepishly, "Or not."

"It's just how it is," he said. "They were famous before I was born. I've never known it any other way."

"Was it weird when you were little? Going to stuff like this?"

"I usually stayed at home with a babysitter. Georgia, too." There was a pause and then, to my surprise, a sudden torrent of words. "We hated the whole paparazzi thing. Photographers would stake out our preschool and hang from trees and yell at us to get our attention—crazy stuff like that. You'd walk out of a building and be blinded by flashes. My sister used to put her hands over her face and cry, she'd be so overwhelmed. One guy actually tried to get her to hold this vodka bottle he'd brought, so he could snap her picture holding it. She was seven."

"That's awful." I was beginning to understand why Derek came off as so standoffish. If you had to deal with strangers constantly getting in your face, rooting for you to mess up in some way so they could get a photo of it, you'd probably learn to be on your guard all the time. And the way some of the kids were at school—all sycophantic and fawning—probably just made him feel even more targeted.

And then there were the people like me, who assumed he was a jerk just because he was trying to protect himself from all that other stuff and who took pride in snubbing someone so famous.

"Don't worry," he said, misinterpreting my silence. "I won't let anyone bother you tonight."

"It's not that. I think I'm starting to understand a little more what you have to deal with every day. It sucks."

"It's not all bad," he said, as we joined up with Juliana and Chase, who were waiting for us near the theater entrance. "In about ten minutes, we're going to be scarfing down as much free popcorn and Coke as we like. There are perks to my life, you know."

"*To* your life?" Chase repeated, overhearing the last bit. "Derek, your life *is* one big perk. I mean, look at this—" He gestured all around us. "This is the American Dream. And you're living it."

"Yeah," Derek said wearily. "I guess I am."

seventeen

When you're actually walking down a red carpet, the bright lights are blinding, and so are the flashes going off all over the place.

Photographers all around us were calling out, trying to get the attention of anyone who might possibly be a celebrity. The tourists screamed whenever they recognized someone famous.

Derek and I walked together, caught in the glare of the klieg lights and the stares of dozens of strangers. I felt excited, bewildered, important, unreal. . . .

Someone said, "Hey, you! Girl in the slip dress!" and I turned toward the voice, without even thinking about it. A light flashed in my face. "Who are you?" the same voice called.

I hesitated, but Derek firmly propelled me forward. "Just ignore them," he said.

A photographer leaned forward over the velvet ropes

that separated us from them and shouted, "Hey, you're Melinda's son, right?" but Derek didn't respond, just kept steadily walking.

Juliana and Chase were right behind us. A voice yelled, "Hey, you—girl with the dark hair in the blue skirt!" I glanced back to see Juliana turn instinctively toward the speaker, and then the same guy screamed at her, "Get out of the way—you're blocking my photo! Brooke, stop! Look here!"

Brooke Shields was right behind Juliana and Chase.

Juliana sped up, tugging Chase forward, and they caught up to us as we entered the building.

"That was so embarrassing!" she said, collapsing against Chase's side and hiding her face in his shoulder.

"Don't let them get to you," Derek said. "Those guys make a living out of being professional jerks."

"Should we find our seats?" Chase asked, glancing around the crowded lobby. A few feet away from us, Megan Fox was talking to a woman in a glittery metallic dress, while a cameraman aimed a handheld video cam at her face.

Derek shook his head. "I should check in with my folks first. They said they'd be doing interviews inside the lobby."

Juliana suddenly detached herself from Chase's side and grabbed my arm. "Look!" she whispered. "That guy over there. See? He was on that Disney show we used to watch. We had the biggest crush on him—remember?"

"Is he wearing eyeliner?" I said. "Yuck."

"I know. And those pants . . . they're practically spray-painted on."

"This is all very disillusioning."

"There they are." Derek pointed across the room. "Come on." He led the way as Chase, Juliana, and I followed in single file along the path he cleared through the crowd to the other end of the lobby, where a more organized interview situation was taking place. Several people were standing against the wall, chatting comfortably like the reporters were old pals and they hadn't even noticed there were microphones and cameras pointed at them.

I recognized all three actors—Johnny Wall, Bud Depatillo, and Melinda Anton . . . aka Derek's mother.

I stared at Melinda Anton as we came closer. It was weird how much I felt like I already knew her. Everything about her face was so familiar: the beauty spot near her lips, the large luminous blue eyes, the unusually arched eyebrows, the cheekbones any woman in America would kill for—and which Derek had inherited, come to think of it.

She felt like an old family friend, like an aunt or a cousin, like someone I had spent hours and hours of my life with. Which I guess I had, only she was always lit up on a screen and I was always in the dark below, watching her. And of course I didn't know her at all—I only knew the characters she played.

Tonight she was wearing a simple black dress, sleeveless, but tailored so that it skimmed her body and showed off her narrow waist and slender legs. Her layered hair looked artlessly messy—which probably meant it had been painstakingly styled by a pro. At first I didn't think she was wearing much makeup at all, but up close I decided she was, it was just skillfully applied.

She was even more beautiful in real life than she was on the screen.

She spotted her son and blew him a kiss. "I'm almost done," she called gaily to him. "Don't go anywhere." Then she glanced around, saying, "Kyle?"

A man immediately removed himself from a nearby group of people and came toward us.

"Hi, Dad," Derek said.

"There you are," said Kyle Edwards. "Did you kids find parking?"

Wow, was that the kind of question movie stars asked their kids? It was so . . . boring.

Derek nodded. "Yeah, no problem."

His father was casual in a T-shirt and jeans, but the unzipped leather jacket he wore somehow made him look carelessly elegant at the same time. He was handsome, and if it hadn't been for a few creases near his eyes and a slight puffiness under them, you'd think he was still in his twenties. His eyes were just like Derek's: gorgeous, dark, veiled in a way that made it impossible to know what he was thinking, but also made you want to find out. His light brown hair was slightly overgrown and stylishly greasy from product. "Chase! How's it going, man?" he said, shaking hands with his son's friend. He turned to Juliana, who nervously sidled closer to me. "And who's this?"

Chase introduced us and Kyle shook first her hand and then mine, gazing into our eyes with an intensity that made me shiver. "Do you also go to Coral Tree?"

Juliana just looked at me, so I had to answer for us both. "Yes. We're new this year."

"Here I am!" a voice trilled. And there she was indeed: Melinda Anton, shoving her hair out of her eyes with a pretty gesture and gently pushing her husband to the side so she could enter our little circle. "Sorry about that. I'm done. For now. Chase!" she exclaimed, giving him a kiss on the cheek. "I'm so glad you came tonight. You always bring the fun."

"Oh, no!" he said with mock distress. "I left the fun in my car. Shall I run and go get it?"

"Didn't your parents teach you to always keep a spare fun in your pocket?" she said, laughing. She turned toward Juliana and me. "Derek," she said, but she was looking at us—my God, those beautiful eyes, that gorgeous face, all aimed at us! "Introduce me to your friends."

"Juliana and Elise Benton," he said. "This is my mother, Melinda Anton." Like we might not know that.

She pressed our hands warmly. "You're sisters? Which one of you is older?"

"I am," Juliana said faintly.

"She's a senior," Chase added. "Like me and Derek." He nudged Juliana's shoulder gently with his.

Melinda registered that and then looked at me with sudden interest.

And I knew why. Chase's affectionate bonk had made it clear that he and Juliana were there as a couple. Which maybe meant I was Derek's date. Her *son's* date.

I flushed under her scrutiny and felt like I was about two years old. The slip dress that had seemed so elegant back at the house now seemed juvenile compared to the severe lines of her simple linen dress. "And you?" she said in her deliciously throaty voice. "What grade are you in, Elise?"

"Eleventh."

"So you don't have to worry about college yet."

"Don't have to, but I do—I'm an early action worrier," I said.

She acknowledged my attempt at a joke with a gracious smile. "Do you have any other siblings?"

"Two more sisters."

"Wow!" Her beautifully arched eyebrows soared

up. "All girls in your family?"

"Yes—I think my parents are still surprised that not a single boy snuck in there."

"They should adopt one from a Third World country," she said seriously. "It's such a wonderful thing to do—you literally save a life."

Yeah, right. I could just picture my mother, Madonna, and Angelina Jolie all trooping off to Malaysia together and becoming besties on the way.

A woman in a navy business suit approached us. "Melinda, Lauren from E! Entertainment says she hasn't gotten any time with you yet."

"Sorry. I'm coming." She ran her fingers quickly through her hair, twisting the ends and arranging the locks carefully so that they appeared to fall carelessly. "Excuse me, kids. I wish I could stay and chat, but I'm working tonight."

"I'm not," Kyle said cheerfully.

"Actually," the woman in the suit told him, "they'd like to do some photos with both of you."

He shrugged in a becomingly self-deprecating way, then carefully ran *his* fingers through *his* hair and minutely adjusted his leather jacket on his shoulders. "Well, then," he said. "Let's go."

Melinda took his arm. As they moved off, she called over her shoulder, "We won't be sitting together, but I hope to see you all at the party."

Party? Juliana mouthed at me. I smiled and shook my head. I hadn't realized there was going to be a party, either. Cool.

We snagged some popcorn and soda—there were rows of both out on the counter, free for the taking, just as Derek had promised—then Chase and Juliana headed up the stairs to the balcony where their seats were. Derek and I were sitting downstairs. We were squeezing through the crowd to get to the entrance of the auditorium when Derek exchanged a brief nod with some guy who was passing us.

He immediately stopped and said, "Derek! How great to see you!"

The guy was fairly handsome with lots of wavy hair that looked dyed and tanned skin that also looked dyed. Hard to tell how old he was. Somewhere between forty and death. "Wow, you've gotten tall!" he said, shaking Derek's hand. "I haven't seen you in years, not since I worked with your mom on *Slippery Slope.* You barely came up to my knees back then."

"How are you?" Derek asked politely.

"Good, good. You still have that stamp collection?"

Derek's smile grew even more strained. "I can't believe you remember that."

"You should keep it up. It's good to have a hobby."
Derek made a noncommittal sound. "You know, my
son is just a couple of years older than you," the guy
said. "Our families should get together—I think you
two would really hit it off."

"Sounds great," Derek said. "Excuse us." He took
my arm, and we moved toward the auditorium entrance.

"Who was that?" I asked.

"No idea. Probably some D-list actor who begged his
agent to get him an invitation. It's the story of my life—
everyone knows who I am because of my parents, but
I never know who they are." His hand was warm and
steady under my arm. "It's my mistake for letting him
make eye contact with me."

"Really? You can't make eye contact with people?"

"Not out in public. The second you do, people see it
as an invitation to start talking to you."

"Is it so bad to have to talk to people?"

"Not always, but a lot of people are nuts and think
they actually know my mom and dad because they've
seen them in movies and read about them in the tabloids,
so they'll say really personal things. And my parents
have to be polite to everyone or suddenly they're known
as the rudest stars in Hollywood. The easiest thing is
just not to open the door to a conversation."

"I get that." We were stuck in a bottleneck of

people waiting to get inside. I took a sip of my Diet Coke. "Well, now I have to ask—"

"What?"

"A stamp collection, Derek? Really?"

He cringed. "Just stick the knife in and twist it around, why don't you? I was, like, six. And it was Jackie's idea—my nanny. Since my parents were always filming in various exotic locations, it gave us something to look for wherever we went."

"So did you score some Australian stamps this summer?"

"Oh, damn, I forgot," he said sarcastically. We had made it through the entryway, but as we headed down the aisle we got stuck behind two young women in absurdly tight and very similar short black dresses who had stopped to hug each other with excited squeals. Idly watching them, Derek said, "Now we only travel during school vacations, but when George and I were little our parents would pull us out of school and take us all over the world with them. Jackie always came along. She's great." He glanced around the bustling auditorium. "Mom invited her tonight, but she's not really into this stuff—she'd only come if George or I begged her to."

"How long has she been your nanny?"

"She's always been my nanny," he said. "Although I hate that word—it sounds so stupid. I don't know what else to call her, though. She was around all the time, took us to the park and the doctor, got us ready for bed, helped us with homework. . . ."

The word for that is mom, I thought. "Was it fun or overwhelming?" I asked. "All that traveling?"

"Both. Georgia and I saw amazing things, but it meant we weren't around other kids much. Made us closer than most siblings but also probably a little—" He searched for the word. "—socially inept, I guess." He shot a grin at me. "You don't disagree with that, do you?"

"Yeah, *that's* not an awkward question," I muttered, and thus managed to avoid answering it.

The girls in the tight dresses finally separated, and we were able to continue down the aisle.

When we got to our row, we had to squeeze past a few people who were already sitting down. I hoped my butt wasn't too much in anyone's face. Our seats were right in the middle and basically the perfect distance from the screen. I guess when your mother's the star of the movie, you get good seats at the premiere.

My fingers were freezing from holding my Diet Coke; it was a relief to put it in the cup holder. Derek offered me some popcorn from the bag he was holding, and I reached in greedily.

"It all seems so cool from the outside," I said.

"What does?"

"The whole celebrity thing. I mean, the traveling and the red carpet and all. . . . But now I know it's got its dark side. Do you ever wish your parents weren't so famous?"

He shrugged. "I've never known it any other way. It's like asking me if I wish I had different-colored eyes."

"Do you?"

There was a short pause. "Sometimes I wish I had blue eyes," he said. "Girls seem to trust guys with blue eyes more."

My chest contracted at that. "Only the stupid ones." I twisted toward him so I could put my hand on his arm. "I'm so sorry. I was wrong about everything. You should hate me. Why don't you hate me?"

"I don't know," he said. He stared at my hand on his arm. "Just can't, I guess. I've tried but then—" He stopped. "Anyway, it's not your fault. I've thought a lot about some of the stuff you said to me at Jason's party and then later, when I asked you to the semiformal—"

"Oh God!" I said, with real distress. "Don't think about that! I acted like a total jerk."

"No." He lowered his voice even more. "You were right about a lot of it." He shifted toward me. His knees settled against mine. "You've made me think about this stuff. About how I act around people sometimes."

"But now I understand it better," I said. "I get why you're careful."

"I was definitely brought up to be. Did you know my house is actually two houses? There's a smaller one close to the street and a bigger one in back. I was six when my parents bought the property, and I said to my mother, 'Why are there two houses? Which one will we live in?' and she said, 'The big one is our real house—it's where you and Dad and Georgie and Jackie and I will all sleep and eat and be together. But when other people come over, we'll play with them in the little house.' And when I asked her why we couldn't have one house like everyone else I knew—like we'd had up until then—she said, 'We need to keep our family safe and private.'" He opened his hands. "That's how she thinks. That's how I was taught to think. We have to keep ourselves separate or it's just not safe."

"Do you think she's right about that?"

He shook his head. "Not when keeping yourself safe turns into pathologically shutting other people out."

I was silent for a moment, thinking about that, and then the lights dimmed, so I had to take my hand away from his arm and sit back in my chair. But I could feel his leg against mine and the silence between us wasn't empty—it was filled with thoughts and hopes and a feeling that made me so overwhelmed, I didn't really feel like talking anymore anyway.

Once everyone else was seated, Melinda Anton was escorted down the aisle by her husband. They sat in the row in front of us. She blew Derek a kiss as she made her way to her seat.

Then the theater lights went out completely, and the screen lit up.

I meant to watch the movie carefully so I could talk about it intelligently afterward, but I was too distracted by my thoughts, and the images flickering on the screen never merged into anything coherent.

We were about ten minutes into it when I felt Derek shift next to me. I flashed him a tentative smile, and he reached out—

And took my hand in his.

You wouldn't think the touch of someone's hand could blow your mind. It's nothing, right? People don't write songs and poems about holding hands— they write them about kisses and sex and eternal love. I mean, when you're a little kid, you hold hands with your parents to cross the street. Who's going to write an ode to that?

But when Derek Edwards took my fingers in his and gently pressed them, first all together and then one by one, I felt that touch set off a wave of firing nerves that flowed up my arm and across my body.

We were alone in the dark, even though the enormous theater was filled with probably a thousand people. We were a tiny island in a sea of other people who didn't matter, who had no meaning, who were so stupid, so oblivious, so stuck in their own boring lives that they didn't even notice the huge, momentous, life-shattering event that was taking place right there in row L, between seats 102 and 104.

Derek Edwards was holding my hand.

The world exploded into billions of atoms, and when it rearranged itself, it may have looked the same, but really, it was a Whole New World. I sat there, catching my breath, trying to gauge the enormity of what had just happened to me, wondering if it was bliss or terror I was feeling—

And that's when my cell phone rang.

eighteen

People have suffered worse embarrassments, I guess, but at that moment it didn't seem possible.

Because I have the worst luck in the world, it rang right in the middle of a quiet, conversational scene. I had no idea what was going on plot-wise, since I hadn't been paying attention to anything but the feel of Derek's fingers playing lightly with mine, but Melinda's character appeared to be saying good night to a small boy in pajamas. The music behind them was gentle and slow.

And then suddenly there was this loud blast of a Green Day song. As I snatched my hand from Derek's and dived frantically on the purse sitting at my feet, I cursed myself not only for forgetting to turn off my phone but for ever thinking that having a rock music ringtone was cool.

Faces turned toward us. Someone made a shushing

sound, and several woman tsk-tsked at me.

I fished my phone out of my purse and got to the ignore button halfway through the second ring.

I looked up, heart pounding, cheeks burning, to see Melinda Anton staring over her shoulder at me. She gave me one level, unreadable look and then turned back to the screen.

I swallowed hard. Why oh why hadn't I remembered to turn my phone off before the movie started?

And now, unbelievably, a text was coming in, making that bonging/clicking sound—not as bad as a ring but still audible—and I shrank even further into my seat, praying Melinda Anton hadn't heard it. It was from Layla, and the subject line was: *Help! 911! Do NOT ignore this!*

I quickly turned the phone off.

Of course it was Layla. The call must have been from her, too. Who else could manage to publicly embarrass me without even being there?

I was sure she was fine. She was always being melodramatic.

I fidgeted in my seat uneasily, still unable to concentrate on the movie.

Layla knew you should put 911 in a text only if the situation was truly serious. Odds were good she just wanted me to run some money to her for a movie or something like that, but what if it really was some kind of emergency?

Worst-case scenarios flooded my mind. Hadn't there once been a shooting in a Starbucks?

I whispered to Derek, "I'm so sorry, but I'd better go check this out."

It's never good to walk out of a movie theater in the middle of a scene. But walking out on a movie that the entire audience worked on . . . Let's just say I got the sense I might as well keep on walking and forget about coming back.

Out in the lobby, I dialed Layla's number, not knowing whether I wanted her to be okay or have a broken leg.

No, now that I'd completely embarrassed myself for her, I definitely wanted her to have a broken leg. Maybe two of them.

She answered instantly. "Elise? Thank God! Juliana's not answering her phone." She didn't sound like she was in pain.

"That's because we're at the movie premiere. Which is why—"

"You've got to help me, Elise. I'm locked in a bathroom in Campbell's house."

That didn't sound good. "Why? What's wrong?"

"It's Webster—he's being so weird."

"Webster? Did you just say Webster? As in Webster Grant?"

"Yeah. He and these stoner friends of his—some rando named Nick and some emo girl he knows—they're all doing stuff, Lee-Lee, like pills and alcohol. And Webster wanted me and Campbell to take stuff, too, and she did but I didn't want to and they were all acting so friggin' weird that I locked myself in here and I don't know what to do now!" Her voice rose into a wail.

"Wait, wait," I said. "Slow down. What about Campbell's parents? Where are they?"

"They're not here, that's the whole point. That's why Webster wanted to come here. He said he wanted to see what Campbell's house was like and then he invited those friends and they all, like, started going through her parents' medicine cabinets and liquor cabinet and stuff. I told them we shouldn't be doing that, but they did anyway."

"Did you know you were meeting these other kids tonight when you went to Starbucks?"

"Webster and Campbell are sort of going out," she said, not exactly answering the question. "At least *she* thinks they are. She's, like, totally into him—she'll do whatever he says—but I don't think he really likes her. He always talks to me more than he does to her." Her voice got very small. "Elise, I can't tell Mom and Dad about any of this. They'll ground me forever. Will you come and get me? Please?"

Good-bye, exciting Hollywood premiere. "I'll try,"

I said, and headed up the lobby stairs. "Chase drove us here, but maybe he'll let me borrow his car. What's Campbell's address?"

"No idea. Can't you, like, track my phone or something?"

"I'm not the FBI. Look, hold on—I need to get Juliana." I opened the door to the balcony. People nearby stared at me, but at least I knew that Melinda Anton was safely downstairs and out of earshot.

The movie was on a night scene, so it was almost pitch-black at first, but then it switched to daytime, which gave off more light, allowing me to locate Juliana and Chase. I crept down the aisle. Fortunately, Chase was right on the end. I tapped him on the shoulder, and they both turned. Juliana looked surprised and then concerned. I gestured silently toward the door, and they followed me back into the hallway just as Derek appeared at the top of the stairs.

I filled them all in as briefly as I could—no details, just that Layla was locked in Campbell's bathroom because she was nervous about how Webster Grant and his friends were behaving.

When I said "Webster Grant," Derek started and made a small sound at the back of his throat.

The other three insisted on leaving with me. I didn't think Derek should walk out on his mother's movie premiere, but he said he'd have plenty of other opportunities to see it and wouldn't let me talk him out of it.

He and I sat together in the backseat of Chase's car.

"This girl—Campbell McGill—it's her bad luck to have a famous dad," he said to me quietly, while the other two were plugging Campbell's address into the GPS system. Chase had used his phone to look it up on the school directory.

"It's my fault," I said morosely. "I introduced them."

"It's not your fault," he said. "I bet he was just waiting for a chance to meet her, and if you hadn't provided one, he would have found some other way to get to her."

"Maybe. But then why did he start hanging out with *me*? My parents aren't famous."

"I'm guessing he just liked you," Derek said. "Can't blame him. For that."

The toneless female GPS voice guided us along Sunset and then north up a narrow windy canyon road to a monstrously large house. There were no outdoor lights on, but there were a couple of cars parked on a big concrete slab in front of the house, and a few of the windows were lit behind closed shades.

I called Layla's cell as we were getting out of the car. "We're here. Where's the bathroom?"

"Upstairs. You go up and then left and it's on the right."

"Stay in there. We'll come get you."

Chase was already ringing the doorbell.

"Wait," Juliana said. "Let them just see me at first. Go stand down there." Chase ducked down below her, into the shadows, and Derek and I lingered several yards behind.

The door opened. "Hi!" Juliana said brightly to the teenage girl who was peering blearily out at her.

"Who're you?" the girl asked, her speech slurred. Her heavily lidded eyes were so smeared with black eyeliner that she looked more like a raccoon than the goth vampiress she was probably trying to channel, given her long black dress and dyed black hair.

"This is Campbell's house, right?"

"Um . . . yeah, I guess."

"Great." As Juliana pushed past her, the rest of us sprang up onto the steps and slipped into the house with her.

The girl was so wasted that she just kind of blinked at us slowly and then let the door close. When I was on the other side of her, I could see that her dress was undone in the back, the zipper open and gaping. Classy.

The foyer was huge, with an entirely white marble floor, a soaring high ceiling, and a wide grand staircase spread out in front of us. The whole effect was spectacularly ugly, like a Barbie Dream House minus the pink.

A guy appeared from behind the stairway. He looked

vaguely familiar—I was pretty sure I'd seen him around school. He moved slowly, planting his feet with excessive caution like he couldn't trust them to work right. Which he probably couldn't.

"Who're they?" he asked the girl, whose head was slowly bobbing up and down like she was finding it hard not to fall asleep right there on her feet. She managed an uneven shrug.

Juliana said, "We'll get Layla," and she and Chase headed up the stairs.

"Where's Campbell?" I asked the couple. I could feel Derek behind me, solid and big. I liked knowing he was back there.

"Who?" the boy said.

The girl seemed a little more aware that something was wrong—or maybe whatever drugs they'd taken had more of a paranoia-inducing effect on her than on the guy. "We should go," she said to him. "Come on—let's get outta here."

I could hear Juliana and Chase knocking on a door upstairs and the faint sound of Layla's voice in response.

"Neither of you should be driving right now," Derek said to the girl.

She just tugged the boy closer to the front door.

There were voices coming from one of the hallways, one giggling and high, one low and barely audible. Derek and I exchanged a glance, then moved quickly in that direction, passing several dark and empty rooms on the way, each one more enormous than the next. Toward the end of the hallway, light shone from under a closed door and the voices were clearer.

The guy was saying, "Pretend it's like a screen test for a movie." The girl said something in response that I couldn't catch.

"In here," Derek said, and put his hand on the bright brass knob.

When we opened the door, Campbell, who was on the sofa, squealed and grabbed for a nearby throw, which she quickly pulled over herself, but not before I'd gotten a glimpse of her bra-only-covered chest.

Her companion had been crouching a couple of feet away, aiming a small Flip digital camera in her direction, but he rose to his feet as soon as I entered. "Oh, hey, Layla," he said. "There you are." Then he shook his head, like he was trying to clear it. "Not Layla," he said. "You guys just look a lot alike. Don't they look a lot alike?" he asked Campbell, who was clutching the throw and pushing herself deep into the sofa cushions.

She looked a little like a trapped animal cowering there, her small eyes darting back and forth between us. She didn't answer.

"Elise!" Webster hit on my name with relief. "Your sister's upstairs. But you didn't need to come pick her up—I was planning on driving her home." As he came closer, I could see that his pupils were dilated and the hair on his temples was matted with sweat. I felt a wave of repulsion so strong, I wanted to throw up. Had I really thought he was cute? There was something fer-rety and shrewd about his face. Why hadn't I noticed that before?

Webster gave a low whistle when he noticed Derek. "Is this your ride, Elise? Nice work! You've done very well for yourself. Congratulations, my love."

Suddenly, from right next to me, Derek sprang—so fast, I didn't see it coming. He grabbed Webster by the shoulders and hauled him in one swift movement up against the wall where he shoved his forearm hard against Webster's throat. Webster struggled to push his arm away, but Derek was too strong and too angry. Webster's feeble flailing at him—hampered by the small video camera he was gripping in his fist—barely even seemed to register.

"Don't you *ever* call her your love," Derek said in a low voice. "You got that?"

"Whoa." Webster's voice was hoarse from the pres-sure at his throat. He held up his hands in a gesture of surrender and rasped out, "Whatever you say, big guy. I never argue with anyone who's got fifty pounds on me."

"You're a piece of shit," Derek said. "I should tear

you apart and make the world a better place."

"Go ahead." Webster freed his hand enough to toss the Flip in Campbell's direction. It landed on the sofa a few inches from her. "Record this, will you, Campby? Melinda Anton's son flies into murderous rage. You know how much money I could get for video of that? Oh, shit." The swear was because I had darted forward and grabbed the Flip before Campbell had even registered that he expected her to pick it up.

Derek removed his forearm from Webster's throat— but only so he could use both hands to slam him against the wall again. "You don't know when to shut up, do you?"

"Just keep going," Webster gasped, his body flopping in Derek's grip. "The worse I look, the more valuable the after photos will be."

But Chase was suddenly in the room, hauling Derek off Webster, Juliana and Layla close behind him. "Come on, D," Chase said. "Don't."

Derek let Chase pull him back, but he didn't take his eyes off Webster, who crouched warily against the wall, catching his breath.

"You okay?" I asked Layla.

"I'm fine," she said impatiently. "Really. You guys are making way too big a deal of this. Sorry about all this," she added to Webster.

"'Sorry'?" I repeated. "You're sorry? Two minutes ago he had you so terrified, you were locked in the bathroom!"

"I don't know why," Webster said, his voice still hoarse. "I would never hurt you, Layla." He caught her gaze and held it. Her eyes softened.

Campbell said, "What's going on? Were you really locked in the bathroom, Layla? Which one?"

Layla said plaintively, "You guys were acting so weird. You were taking pills."

"My mom takes them all the time," Campbell said. "And she's fine." She was still curled up on the sofa, clutching the blanket to her upper body, her pretty layered hair fanning out on the cushions all around her. "Anyway, I only took one little Vicodin. You're such a baby." She looked up at Derek hopefully. "Everything's okay here, but you can stay if you want to. We have beer."

"Oh, great," he said with an ominous look at Webster. "Weren't you leaving, Grant?"

"Yeah," Chase agreed. "He was."

"We were having fun," Campbell said. "Layla, tell them to let him stay."

"Yeah, guys, let him stay," Layla said. "It's her house, you know. I shouldn't have called you. I had no idea you were going to embarrass me like this."

"Oh, for God's sake, shut up!" Juliana turned on her with more rage than I'd ever seen before from my gentle sister. "Embarrass you? You're acting like a five-year-old!"

"Poor Layla," Webster said sympathetically. "That's the thing about big sisters—you'll always be a baby to them."

"I know!" she said. I saw how she was already opening up to him again, and it made me sick. She and Campbell were defenseless against Webster's charm. I was two years older, and *I'd* fallen for it.

"We'll walk you to your car," Chase said to Webster.

"I can get there by myself."

"Then do it."

"May I have my camera back first?" He held out his hand toward me. I hesitated. He said pleadingly, "It cost me two hundred bucks, Elise. I can't afford to lose it."

"Fine." I turned it on, and a picture of a coyly draped Campbell popped up on the screen.

"Hold on," Webster said. "Don't delete anything—"

"Oops," I said as I punched the buttons that deleted everything. "Too late." I handed the Flip back to him.

"My grandparents' fiftieth wedding anniversary was on there," he said sadly. He shoved it in his pocket. "Those memories are gone forever."

"Take more at the sixtieth," I suggested.

"I didn't expect *you* to act like this, Elise." He stepped

toward me, his keen blue eyes searching my face for something—maybe some trace of sympathy. "I thought we were friends."

"That's funny," I said. "I thought you were decent."

nineteen

"That was totally humiliating," Layla complained as we drove away. She was crammed in the back between me and Derek. "All I wanted was a ride home, but you had to turn it into this whole big scene. I'll never be able to face my friends again."

No one responded.

"Don't tell Mom and Dad about the pills, okay?" Layla said after a moment, in a more conciliatory tone. "They'll ground me, you know they will, even though *I* didn't take anything. And it's not like anything bad actually happened."

"Oh, for God's sake," Derek growled from his side of the car.

"No offense," Chase said to Juliana, "but your little sister is a moron."

"I know," she said wearily. "So's yours." There was a pause, and then suddenly the two of them were giggling.

And then I was, too. And finally, even Derek's taut face relaxed into a smile.

It was still surprisingly early when Chase dropped the three of us off at home, only about nine thirty. So much had happened that it felt like it should have been closer to midnight.

I tried to catch Derek's eye as we all got out of the car, but Mom was opening the front door and heading toward us, so I couldn't blame them when he and Chase murmured hasty good-byes and jumped back in the car.

I walked slowly up the walkway after my sisters, feeling depressed. The evening that had started out so happily had turned totally awkward. Story of my life.

We met Mom halfway to the house. "Why did they take off so quickly?" she asked as Chase's car disappeared around the corner. "And how did you end up with Layla? Your father was staying awake just so he could get her."

"She called us," Juliana said, like that explained everything.

"I thought the premiere would go later," Mom said to me. "Did you meet Melinda Anton?"

"Briefly."

"What was she like?"

"She seemed nice." I so didn't feel like talking.

She followed us inside. "Why didn't the boys come in with you? It's dark out and I don't like you girls walking up to the house alone." She closed the door and turned around, seeing us in the light for the first time. "Especially dressed like that!" She crossed her arms. "I have underwear that covers me more than that dress, Elise."

That's when I realized I'd left my jacket in the trunk of Chase's car.

"Did you think I wouldn't notice that you left the house with more clothing than you had on when you returned?" Mom shook her head crossly. "No wonder the boys dropped you off so early."

"What's that supposed to mean?" I asked, stepping out of my shoes right there in the hallway. My feet were killing me.

"Maybe they're wondering if you're who they thought you were."

"Oh, for God's sake," I said. "We had to pick up Layla, that's all."

"At least *she* looks decent." She turned to Layla, who had quickly tightened the drawstring neck of her shirt before entering the house. "You should give your older sister a lesson in what's appropriate."

"Any time." Layla eyed me contemptuously. "She could definitely use my help."

"Oh, yes," I said. "I want to be guided by you because you are so wise."

"There's no need to be sarcastic," Mom said.

"Isn't there?" I said sarcastically.

A little while later, I was lying on my bed, staring miserably up at the ceiling. "Nothing ever goes right for me."

"Poor Lee-Lee." Juliana sat down next to me and patted my arm. We were alone in our room. "It's not that bad. I know we had to leave the movie, but at least you and Derek—"

"Don't," I said. "You're making it worse."

"Why? You like him a little now, don't you?"

"That's the problem." I rolled off the bed and went over to my dresser. I found a sweatshirt and pulled it on over my dress. I hadn't realized how cold I was until now, when all the excitement had died down. But the fact that I had spent the last few hours in fifty-degree weather wearing nothing more than a slip had caught up to me, and I was suddenly freezing. "I do like him now. A lot. But tonight ruined everything. Being dragged into Layla's mess like that and then to have her act like such an ingrate . . ." I wished I could tell Juliana why Webster's involvement made it so bad for Derek, but I couldn't.

"That doesn't matter," Jules said. "Layla isn't you. I mean, I hate Chelsea, but I like Chase."

"He barely said good night, Jules. He just wanted to leave as quickly as possible."

"Because it was awkward with all of us there. And you can't blame him for wanting to avoid talking to

Mom. Chase left just as fast, you know."

"Why can't our family be normal?" I moaned. "Other than you, I mean?"

"No one's family is normal. Normalcy is a lie invented by advertising agencies to make the rest of us feel inferior." She yawned. "I'm exhausted. I don't have the energy to do anything useful—want to watch some TV?"

Down in the family room, Layla was already deep into some show about girls in a private prep school who were so rich they could change into a different designer outfit every ten minutes—which I would have thought was total fiction a year earlier, but now, after I'd spent a couple of months at Coral Tree, practically played like a documentary.

Juliana and I squeezed onto the sofa next to Layla. It was cramped, but I'll give my sisters this: they're warm and cozy on a cool night.

"What's that?" Layla said a little while later, lunging for the remote. She paused the TV and cocked her head, listening. "Is that a knock?" She threw down the remote and jumped off the sofa and was out the door in a flash. We followed close behind, curious: we never got guests at that hour.

My parents appeared on the stairs just as we all reached the front door. "What on earth—?" Mom said.

She was wearing a pink nightgown with a blue flannel bathrobe. My father had on paisley pajamas. They both looked ridiculous.

Layla opened the door. "Oh, it's you again," she said. "Why'd you come back?"

Derek Edwards was standing on the front step, his head thrust forward awkwardly. His eyes connected with mine over Layla's shoulder. "You left this in the car," he said, holding out my jacket. "I thought you might need it."

I reached past Layla. "Thank you," I said. "Sorry you always have to return my clothes. Okay, that sounded really wrong."

"That's very nice of you, Derek," my mother said. She wasn't wearing her glasses, so she must have already gone to bed, but she didn't seem annoyed about being woken up. She tied her bathrobe a little tighter and took a step down. "Why don't you come on in and we'll make some tea?"

"Thanks, but I was wondering . . . my mom's premiere party is still going on. Maybe—if it's okay with you—Elise could run over there with me for a few minutes?" His eyes darted up toward my parents, then back toward me, questioningly. "We don't have to stay long."

"I'd love to," I said, just as my father said gruffly, "It's a little late to be heading out, Elise."

"It's not that late," I said quickly. "I'll be home before one, I promise. And it's Saturday night, so no worries about getting my homework done—I can work all day tomorrow. And I'll be really quiet when I come home so I don't wake anyone up. Bye!" I crammed my feet back into the Shoes of Pain, glad I had left them right there, slipped out the door, and closed it before my father had a chance to tell me I couldn't go.

Derek looked a little stunned. "Come on!" I said, dragging him down the walkway.

As we got into his car, he said, "Why do I feel like the getaway driver for a crime?"

"Sorry, but they might not have let me go if they'd had more time to think about it."

He nodded and started the car. "I feel bad," he said after a moment. "I meant to invite your sister to come with us, but we left so quickly. . . ."

"It's okay. I mean, I love Juliana—"

"I've noticed."

"—but it's nice to have some time with just us."

"I know," he said. "We haven't had much of that."

I cautiously checked his face and, to my huge relief, didn't see any lingering anger or resentment there. "What if we get really bored now that we're alone together?" I said lightly. "Wouldn't that be sad?"

"I'm bored already." He grinned sideways at me.

"Where's Chelsea Baldwin when you need her?"

"She takes me to my happy place," he agreed.

I laughed. But something still worried me. "Do you think your mother will be mad at me? For leaving the movie and making you leave, too?"

"I texted her that you had a family emergency. She'll understand—she's very rah-rah about family sticking together."

"Really? That doesn't fit with my image of a big movie star."

"My parents aren't always around," he said. "But in some ways I think that makes the idea of family even more important to them. They can go out and do the whole industry thing knowing that when they go home, they get to be a mom and dad again."

"But they sent Georgia to boarding school."

"They didn't want to. It was just . . . the right choice."

We were both quiet then. "We should do something about him," I said after a moment. "Get him kicked out of school at least. If I told my mother—"

He shook his head. "It's complicated, Elise. His grades are decent, he hasn't been caught doing anything, and Georgia won't talk about what happened to her. And Campbell McGill is a moron."

"If he actually sold some photos and they could trace them back to him—"

"Then you'd have something to throw him out over." He sighed. "But whoever's in the photo would be publicly humiliated first, so let's hope he doesn't."

"You know what?" I said abruptly. "I don't want to talk about Webster Grant anymore. Or about your mother. Or about *my* mother. Or about any sisters, fathers, dogs, uncles, aunts—"

Derek said, "We can always talk about the weather."

"We live in L.A.," I said. "We don't have weather. Nothing to talk about."

"That works out nicely," he said, glancing at the GPS. "Since we're almost there."

twenty

The party was at a restaurant in Beverly Hills that had a nondescript exterior and no signage. The windows were shuttered. The only way to tell we were even in the right place was the small notice on the valet parking stand that had the restaurant's name next to the seven-dollar (!) parking fee.

Derek was coming around the front of the car to join me on the sidewalk when he did a double take. "I didn't really get a good look at you before. What exactly are you wearing, Elise?"

I looked down and realized I was still wearing a maroon UMass Amherst athletic hoodie over my slip dress and high heels. "You don't like my outfit?" I pretended to be hurt.

"It's fine," he said uncertainly.

"I'm teasing," I said. "I totally look like a crazy woman."

"I kind of like it."

"Yeah, right." I told the valet who was getting in the car to hold on a sec and opened the passenger door again, pulled off the sweatshirt, and tossed it inside.

I closed the door and smoothed out my dress. "Come on," I said, and, without even thinking about it, reached my hand out to Derek.

He instantly took it, and the touch of his large, warm hand made me take a sudden sharp breath. "You okay?" he said, misunderstanding. "Too cold? You want your crazy-lady sweatshirt back?"

"I'm fine," I said, and held on tight.

The restaurant was bigger inside than I'd expected and filled with people, noise, and vibrating lights. We stopped to get our bearings, but I can't say I succeeded at that.

"You hungry?" Derek asked.

"A little."

"I'm starving." We were on our way over to the food tables when Derek suddenly stopped and reached into his pocket. He squinted down at his phone. "It's my mom. She said she's at a booth near the kitchen. . . ." He scanned the room. "There she is. Come on. We'll just say hi. We don't have to stay long."

As we approached, Melinda stood up and Derek gave her a casual peck on the cheek.

It still amazed me to see them together. How could he live with Melinda Anton, have breakfast with her, ask her for allowance, and tell her he had banged up the car?

She held her hand out to me and I took it. "Thanks for letting me come to this."

"My pleasure." She pressed my fingers but didn't let go. "Derek told me you had some sort of family emergency. I hope everything's all right?"

"I'm so sorry we had to leave early." My palm was growing sweaty in her grasp. I wanted to wipe it off on my dress, but she wouldn't release it. "I—it was my sister. My younger sister. She . . .We just had to go get her really suddenly. The movie was great. I wouldn't have left except . . . you know . . . she said it was an emergency." Could I have sounded any more idiotic?

"Is she okay?"

"She's fine. She really just needed a ride, but she made it sound urgent."

"Ah." She seemed genuinely relieved. "Well, we'll have to arrange for you to see the rest of the movie sometime."

"I'd like that."

"Melinda!" A thin woman with enormous breasts that were struggling to escape her halter dress leaned forward to grasp Melinda's forearms. "You were brilliant!" she sang out. She stretched over the table to kiss

Melinda on the cheek, putting her boobs in serious danger of popping out all the way. "I cried and cried. It took me half an hour to redo my mascara." She twisted to look at me and Derek. "Wasn't it *wonderful*? Have you ever seen anything so *moving*?" Since I hadn't seen most of the movie, I couldn't really answer her. Fortunately, she didn't wait for an answer, just turned back to Melinda. "I'd love to see you revisit this character one day—she's so strong, so brilliant, so *you*. There'll be an Oscar campaign, no?"

"Don't even," Melinda said, laughing and extricating her hands.

The pudgy middle-aged man sitting down next to Melinda said, "She's right. It's your time, sweetie. We all know it." He was wearing a blue beret. Really. A beret.

"Let's not talk about it. I don't want to jinx anything. I'm very superstitious," Melinda informed me with a charmingly self-deprecating shrug.

"We're going to look for some food," Derek said abruptly.

"There's not much here for us to eat, sweetie. Want me to ask them to make up a fruit plate for you?" With a quick glance around, she skillfully made everyone feel included in the conversation. "Derek's doing the raw food thing with me. We both have so much more energy!" She put her hand to the side of her mouth and said in a stage whisper, "But I suspect he cheats! Sometimes he has pizza breath!"

"Teenagers," said the woman in the halter dress with a smile.

"I know." Melinda reached for Derek's hand. "He leaves me next year," she informed her companions as she cradled it against her cheek. "Can you believe it? He's going to college. 'Somewhere far away from you,' he says whenever we talk about it. He can't wait to leave me."

Derek shifted uncomfortably. "That's not true. I just said I was interested in the East Coast."

"Because it's far from me." She kissed the back of his hand. "Ah, well. Part of being a mother is knowing when to let go."

"He'll come back for vacations," the woman said. "They always do."

"Yeah," the beret said. "They lie around the house, watching TV, making dirty laundry, and eating you out of house and home. You'll be dying for him to leave again."

"And on that note . . ." Derek retrieved his hand. "Excuse us." We said good-bye and headed across the room. It was a relief to walk away.

Melinda Anton was famous and glamorous, but she still had that universal mom ability to embarrass her own child.

As we studied the unappealing platters of sweating

cheese cubes and curling vegetables, Derek gestured back in the direction of his mother and said in a low voice, "Sometimes I just—" But he was interrupted by a very small man with thinning hair who swooped down on us. "Derek Edwards!" he cried out. "How's it going, my friend?" He held his hand up for a high five, but Derek put his own out at shaking height so the guy dropped his hand and they shook. "You know who I am, right? John Montero? I work at your dad's production company. We've met a whole bunch of times. It is so good to see you again! It's been a while. You used to drop by the office a lot more."

"Yeah, well, senior year and all," Derek said. "Nice to see you." He turned back to the table. "So what looks good to you, Elise?"

"The chicken skewers are ah-mah-zing," the guy said before I could answer. "And the caprese salad—to die for! So are you a friend of Derek's?" I gave a brief, tentative nod. "Lucky you. And lucky him, too, I'm sure. I'm sitting with your dad and some other people over in the corner," he said to Derek. "I'm just getting myself a second helping of those heavenly skewers and then I'm heading back over there. Come join us!"

"Actually," Derek said, putting his hand on my back, "Elise needs to get going, don't you, Elise?"

"I'm late already," I agreed obediently.

"Well, don't go before you try the skewers," John Montero said.

"I'm on a raw food diet," Derek said apologetically. Then, to me, "Let's get you home." We headed toward the exit.

"Sorry about leaving so suddenly," he said as we waited for the valet to bring his car. "But I could already tell we weren't going to get left alone for a—" There was a sudden burst of light in my eyes, and I jumped in surprise. "Oh, for God's sake!" he said, and pulled me against him like he was trying to protect me from something.

"What was that?"

"Just a flash," he said grimly. "Paparazzi."

It occurred to me I should probably move away from him—did I really want anyone taking my photo all crushed against Derek's chest like that?—but a slightly dopey feeling of enjoyment was spreading over me at the feel of his jacket under my cheek and his arms wrapped tightly around my shoulders. Part of me just wanted to melt and relax into him. Actually, all of me wanted to do that. Who cared if they took a picture? I wasn't anybody anyway—the worst they could do was print the photo with the caption "Melinda Anton's son and unknown female" under it.

Derek wasn't exactly rushing to push me away, so

we stayed like that, wrapped up in each other, my face hidden against his arm, until he murmured, "My car," and I slid out from his embrace without meeting his eyes, a little embarrassed and a little uncertain what I'd see there.

twenty-one

Once we were settled in his BMW, Derek asked me if I wanted to go to his house.

"Sounds great." I might have sounded a little too eager. But I really wanted to be alone with him at this point—somewhere we could relax. And I knew his parents wouldn't be there.

After we reached Brentwood, we headed north and wound up at a guardhouse, where the guy on duty waved us through an enormous iron gate. Then we turned onto what was either a big driveway or a small road and had to stop at another, somewhat smaller gate that Derek had a remote control for, before we finally parked in front of what I assumed was the Edwards/Anton home.

Once I'd adjusted to the enormity of the property, to how the lawn, trees, and flowering plants stretched on for miles, lit up by random spotlights even at this late hour, and to how the main building—flanked by several smaller connected ones—was wider and went back farther than I could even make out in the dim light, I realized that the house itself was actually kind of simple, in that spare, elegant, modern way that you usually only see in magazines. There was nothing ornate or unnecessary in the design, no swirling ironwork, no little pillars, no windowboxes, just strong, clean lines.

If houses had genders, this one was male. A very handsome male.

The very handsome male at my side said, "What do you think?"

I was suddenly aware I'd been standing there with my mouth open like a fish. (Speaking of which, there was a koi pond not five feet from us, stocked with freakishly large red-gold beauties, whose scales flashed in the spotlight shining down on them.) "It's beautiful." I hesitated, then said uncertainly, "Is this your real house? Or the guest one?"

He laughed. "We passed the guest house on the way in. I'm taking you straight into the belly of the beast. You okay with that?"

"I'm kind of honored."

"Good. Are you cold? Do you want to grab your sweatshirt first?"

I said firmly, "I will die of frostbite before I wear that sweatshirt over this dress again" and headed toward the enormous carved-wood front door, but Derek caught my arm and said, "This way," with a bob of his head toward the side of the house. I followed him around the corner to a small porch.

He pulled keys out of his pocket. "Smile," he said as he unlocked the door.

"Any particular reason?"

He pointed above my head. I looked up and into the round black lens of a security camera bolted to the wall. "You're being filmed," he said, and opened the door.

Inside, he led me down a narrow hallway—"Laundry room, pantry, Jackie's room—" he recited, gesturing at various doorways—and into a large kitchen. There was only one dim counter light on when we entered, but Derek hit another switch and the entire kitchen became bright.

Really bright: everything in the room was white or stainless steel, except for the floor, which was a veined green marble. It was easily the largest kitchen I'd ever been in and had the biggest oven and island I'd ever seen. The far side of the kitchen opened onto a family room with an enormous sectional sofa that faced a large-screen TV.

It was all kind of intimidating, but I liked the glass bowl of apples and oranges on the island—real, ripe ones, not old or fake ones—and the vase of sunflowers on the counter near one of the several sinks. It felt like someone had made an effort to warm up the otherwise antiseptic and oversized space.

"Let's see what we have to eat." Derek flung open one of three gargantuan floor-to-ceiling stainless-steel refrigerators (or freezers?) and studied its contents. "Have a seat," he added over his shoulder, with a flick of his chin toward the stools that lined one side of the big island.

I perched on a caramel-colored leather seat, leaned forward, and rested my chin on my hands so I could gaze at Derek as he sorted through items in the fridge, free to admire unobserved his strong back and narrow waist and broad—

He turned and caught me staring at him. He cleared his throat and said a little unevenly, "Um, there's not a ton to eat unless you have a craving for wheatgrass or jicama. My mom's still on her crazy diet. But there's fruit and I think we have some chips in the pantry."

"I'm not actually that hungry," I said, because something about the tone of his voice and the way we were alone in the kitchen was making my stomach curl up and shrink in on itself. I was beginning to understand why Juliana stopped eating when she fell in love.

Not that I was falling in love.

Not that I wasn't.

He kicked the fridge door closed with the back of his foot and said, "We might—"

Before he could finish, a small woman suddenly emerged from the back hallway. She stood in the doorway blinking at us from behind owlish black glasses. Her dark hair was pulled back in a long thick braid, and she was wearing a bathrobe over plaid pajamas. Simple leather slippers completed the "at home about to go to bed" look.

"I thought I heard you come in," she said in a brisk English accent. "What are you doing back so early? Figured you'd be at the party until midnight at least. And who's this?"

"This is Elise," Derek said. "Elise, this is Jackie."

Ah. The nanny.

"Nice to meet you," she said, and hustled forward, her hand extended. I slid off the stool and we shook. I felt her scrutinize me and wished—not for the first time that night—that I had worn something more substantial and less revealing than that slip dress. I had dressed for what the evening was supposed to be and not for what it had turned into. She turned to Derek. "Thought you two could sneak in without my hearing, eh?"

"Actually," he said, "I was hoping you'd come help us. We're hungry and there's nothing to eat."

"Oh, and I'm supposed to take care of that for you?" she said with a sort of fond annoyance. "You can't possibly make a little snack for yourself? He's like that, you know," she said to me. "Always inconveniencing others, only thinking of his own needs."

I laughed, and she nodded at me as if to say, *Good for you—you know I'm joking.*

She crossed over to the refrigerator. "Since I'm up anyway, I suppose I could make you something. An omelet? She still lets me buy eggs, you know, even though She won't touch them Herself, not with that crazy diet of Hers." She turned and added in an audible whisper, "And there are pizzas and hamburgers hidden in the freezer, but don't tell Her, or it'll be nuts and berries for us all for the rest of the year."

"Pizza, Elise?" Derek asked me hopefully.

"Sure." I still wasn't hungry, but pizza sounded as good as anything.

"I'll pop it in the oven. Is it asking too much of you to take it out when it's done?" Jackie's small black eyes were shrewd but kind behind those big glasses. The lights were brighter near the refrigerators, and I could see threads of gray in her hair: she wasn't as young as I'd thought at first.

"I think we can manage that," Derek said.

"But I suppose you'll be needing me to chew the crust for you and pass it into your mouth like a mama bird. He's lazy," she said to me. "And selfish. Never lifts a finger to help anyone, never carries a bag of groceries, never stops to chat when I'm feeling lonely, never calls his sister to check up on her. Selfish, selfish, selfish."

Again that seemed to be a joke. Which led me to assume Derek actually helped her a lot, because otherwise it was a lousy joke.

"Do we have any barbecued chicken pizzas left?" Derek asked, peering over her head into the freezer. He was at least a foot taller than she was. "And shouldn't you be preheating the oven?"

"Oh, go away, will you?" she said, shoving him gently. "Unless you want to do it yourself. Why don't you go show your friend the indoor swimming pool and impress her with that since you don't have the looks to get a girl any other way?" She nodded in my direction. "Is she the one you've been telling me about?"

"Shh," he said, hastily turning to me. "Come on, Elise—I'll give you a tour."

He ushered me out of the kitchen and into the family room, then through its open doorway into another hallway, much more formal than the other one, wider and with higher ceilings. There was stained hardwood under our feet, and the walls were painted in neutral colors and hung with large paintings under simple spotlights, like in a museum.

"What was that about?" I asked Derek, pulling him to a halt. "What Jackie just said?"

"She has a big mouth." He avoided my eyes. "That's

the butler's pantry and that's the dining room and that's the—"

I shook my head. "You are so not getting out of this one. I've had to suffer through being embarrassed by my family plenty of times in front of you—now it's your turn. Tell me what she was talking about."

He flushed. "It's nothing." He glanced up and down the hallway, a little desperately. "Fine," he said. "I made the mistake of mentioning to her once that there was a girl at school I liked who didn't like me back. You happy now?"

"And that was me?"

He rocked back on his heels with a deep sigh. "You're a little bit of an idiot, you know that?"

"Did you tell her how rude you were to me at first?" I said. "Or did you make it sound like it was all my fault?"

"All I told her was that I didn't have a chance in hell with you."

"Well then," I said, looking down, feeling my cheeks turn hot, "who's the idiot now?" When I had the courage to glance up at him again, he was grinning.

"Come see the screening room," he said, and took my hand firmly in his, sliding his fingers in between mine. I let him lead me down to the end of the hallway, where he opened a door to reveal a room so huge, it must have run the entire length of the house. There was a large movie screen at the far end, recessed into the wall, and rows of velvet-upholstered reclining arm-chairs and small sofas.

I just stood there, gaping at it. I couldn't believe someone would have this in his home. It was bigger than some movie theaters I'd been in.

"You want to watch something until the pizza's ready?" he asked. "A movie? TV show? Press tour clips of my mother? That's a joke, by the way."

"Not enough time for a movie," I said. "Something short."

"Let me see what we've got."

I moved forward, toward one of the chairs. He caught me by the arm and nodded at a little sofa. "Maybe one of those?" There was a hopeful, almost wistful sound in his voice. It wasn't something you normally heard from Derek Edwards but I liked it.

I sat on the sofa.

He did something with some kind of machinery—I had no idea what. I mean, I noticed the curve of his neck as he bent down, and the way his hair flopped forward so he had to push it out of his eyes, but whether the machine was a projector, a DVD player, Blu-ray . . . I had no idea. Didn't know, didn't care.

Derek picked up a remote and came back to where I sat on the sofa, hugging my arms against my chest, shivering a little with something that wasn't cold.

"Is this seat taken?" he said, joking—but his voice sounded a little shaky. He sat down next to me. The sofa was small, which forced his thigh to press against mine. "I can control everything with this," he said, pointing the remote. "See—" He pressed some buttons and the picture and sound came on. "It controls the lights, too," he said very quietly, and the room slowly grew dark around us, until the only light was coming from the screen.

For a moment we sat there side by side in the dark room, watching Lady Gaga howl and crouch. She wasn't wearing much clothing. I clasped my hands and laid them primly on my lap.

I waited.

And then I felt Derek take a deep breath and shift a little away from me—but only so he could move his arm. As it settled around my shoulders, I relaxed into it and against him and for the second time that night felt the warmth of his cotton-covered chest against my cheek.

The video changed. Lady Gaga went away. Taylor Swift appeared. The music was calmer. I rolled my head back, so I could raise my face toward Derek's. "Don't you think—" I started to say, but the rest of that sentence got blotted out forever, even from my memory, because Derek Edwards chose that moment to lower his face to mine and kiss me.

Finally.

At first his lips were tentative and questioning against mine, but something in my response must have reassured him, because pretty soon his mouth grew more confident and his arms tightened around me until he was almost crushing me against his chest.

And I liked the feeling of being almost crushed, of being so much smaller than him, of his body enveloping mine, and of his mouth hot against my lips.

I got lost in him, and it was the kind of lost that's exactly like being found.

An eternity went by. Or maybe it was a split second.

Hard to be sure, but it occurred to me that the pizza might be burning. I managed to whisper something about that to Derek.

"Let it burn," he murmured, his lips moving against mine in a way that was very distracting, and for a moment I thought, *Yeah, he has a point.*

But no—the house was too nice to burn down, and I pushed him firmly away from me so I could say so.

"It's not that nice," he said, leaning in toward me again. "And we have insurance."

This time, my shove was less gentle. "Bad enough my phone went off at her premiere," I said. "I burn down your house and your mother will never let me near you again. Unless that's your goal?"

"Yeah," he said. "This has all been an elaborate plot to get you out of my life." He sighed and stood up. "Fine. We'll go check on the pizza, since that's so important to you." He held out his hand and helped me get to my feet. "Hold on a sec," he said.

"What?" I looked down, thinking I had some fuzz or something on my dress, but he put his finger under my chin and tilted my head up and kissed me again. It felt different from a standing position. A difference that definitely needed to be explored. So we explored it.

"Pizza?" I whispered after some more time had gone by.

He raised his head slightly. "All you think about is food."

"I'm worried about burning the house down!" I protested.

"See what I mean?" he said. "Food, food, food." And then he lowered his face to mine again.

Somehow, eventually, we did manage to separate long enough to make it to the kitchen, where we found Jackie already cutting up the pizza. "The buzzer went off ten minutes ago," she snapped, looking over her shoulder as we entered. We were holding hands but dropped them sheepishly at the sight of her. "'Oh, yes, we'll take the pizza out of the oven,'" she said in a mincing voice. "'Oh, yes, we'll listen for the buzzer, Jackie. No problem, Jackie. You go on to bed, Jackie, don't worry, we'll take care of everything.'"

"We were in the screening room," Derek said. "It's not our fault it's soundproof."

She shook her head and carried the platter over to the island, which—I now realized as we got closer—she had already set with plates, glasses, silverware, napkins, and a tray of cut-up fresh fruit. "I think you have everything you need." She surveyed the spread. "Do I have your permission to go to sleep now?"

"Please go to bed," Derek said. "Before you embarrass me more."

"I haven't even started." She turned to me. "Next time I'll tell you some stories about him when he was little."

"Difficult?" I said.

"Difficult?" She looked genuinely surprised. "My little Derek? The shyest kid you've ever seen, used to hide in my skirt wherever we went. You couldn't get him to say a word to anyone, and he'd do whatever you told him to. I miss those days. As you can see, he's changed." She waved her hand in the air. "All right, all right, I'm leaving. Lovely to meet you, Elise."

"You too," I said.

She leaned forward and whispered loudly, "Go easy on him. I know you girls today like to torture your young men, but he's a good one."

"Okay," said Derek, whose face had turned bright red. "Now you *really* have to leave." He took her by the shoulders and gently—but firmly—shuttled her tiny body out of the kitchen and into the back hallway. He returned, dusting off his hands.

"So that was Jackie," I said, sitting on a stool and plucking an orange section off the fruit plate.

"That was Jackie," he agreed, sitting down on the stool next to me.

I nibbled on the slice. "She's kind of adorable." I carefully licked a drop of juice from one end of the orange. "Like a cross between a leprechaun and Mary Poppins."

"Do you have any idea how distracting that is?"

It took me a moment to realize he was talking about the way I was tonguing the orange section. "Sorry," I said, and popped it entirely into my mouth.

"No, you're not."

I smiled.

He served himself a slice of pizza. "You going to have any?"

"I'm not all that hungry."

"Have another orange section," he suggested, his eyes gleaming. "I like when you eat those."

"Shut up." I swiveled in my stool so our knees brushed lightly against each other. "I should probably go home as soon as we're done. It's late."

"Can't you stay for a movie?"

"It's already past midnight."

"Really?" He looked at his watch with genuine surprise. "My parents will be home soon."

"Yeah, well, that's another reason right there to get going. I don't think I have the guts to face your mom a third time in one night. Especially since I keep taking you away from her parties. She must hate me."

"She probably didn't even notice we left."

I watched him eat his pizza. He ate neatly, folding up the slice and biting into it sideways so no sauce spilled out. I said, "But I'd like to come back and watch a movie another time."

He sat up, wiped his mouth and fingers with a napkin, took a sip of water, and took his time before leaning back in the stool and lazily regarding me. "Then," he said, "you will."

We pulled up in front of my house half an hour later. I said good-bye and reached for the door.

"That's it?" he said. "That's all I get?"

"Sorry, but if anyone other than Juliana is watching—"

"Got it." He turned the car off. "I'll walk you up to the door, shake your hand, thank you politely for a lovely evening, and deliver you safely into your mother's waiting arms. How's that?"

"You'll be the answer to her dreams."

"Just hers?"

"No, you idiot. Not just hers."

His hand reached for mine and squeezed it hard. "Come on," he said. "Let's go put on our little performance."

But I opened the front door to darkness and silence.

"Can I call you tomorrow morning?" Derek asked from the step below. "Maybe we can meet at a Starbucks, get some homework done?"

"And then find some place to be alone after?" We smiled stupidly at each other for a while, and then I reluctantly stepped back. "You'd better go." I stood in the doorway and watched him get into his car and drive away, amazed that I'd actually gotten to put my hands around that long, strong body and touch my lips to that handsome face, eager to do it again as soon as possible, wishing the hours away until then, happier than I'd felt in ages, maybe ever.

I shook myself awake, stepped all the way inside,

closed the door, turned around . . . and almost screamed.

My mother was standing right behind me in the dark.

How long had she been there?

"It's almost one, Elise." Her tone was unexpectedly mild—she was stating a fact, not reaming me out.

"Sorry." I flicked on the light. "I hope I didn't wake you."

She didn't answer, just leaned forward and sniffed at my mouth. I was used to the alcohol check and obligingly breathed out in her direction. She nodded her approval. (She didn't know it, but she owed me some thanks: that breath would have been a lot more garlicky and less pleasant if I'd eaten the pizza instead of the orange.)

Before she stepped back, I caught a whiff of wine coming from her and was tempted to point out she would have flunked her own test. But she was over twenty-one and, anyway, I kind of preferred my mother after she'd had some wine. It mellowed her out.

"Were you waiting up for me?" I asked.

She shook her head. "I woke up and couldn't sleep, so I thought I'd answer some emails. Parents are always writing me."

"Were there a lot of angry ones?"

"People never write to say things are fine." She played with the belt on her bathrobe for a moment. "So,

Elise, are you and Derek Edwards officially a couple now?" The barely restrained eagerness in her voice disturbed me.

"I don't know." I moved toward the staircase. "We had a nice time together. But it's no big deal."

"Do you like him?"

"I think so."

"That's all I care about, you know. If you girls are happy, I'm happy."

"Good to know." I pretended to yawn, and it turned into a real one. "It's been a crazy night," I said. "I'm exhausted."

"Did you get a chance to talk to them more?" she asked idly, following me to the stairs. "Derek's parents?"

"I talked to Melinda a little." I put my foot on the bottom step.

"Did she ask you about me?" She curled around the banister, so she could look up into my face. "Does she know your mother's the school principal?"

"We didn't get that far."

"Maybe I should invite them over," she said. "You know how Dad and I like to meet the parents of your friends. I could see if Derek's parents could join us for a barbecue one weekend."

I stared at her. "Are you crazy?"

She drew herself up. "Why not? Just because people star in movies doesn't make them superior to the rest of us, you know. As the principal of a high school, I also affect a lot of lives."

Great. I'd hurt her feelings. Damage control time. "I just meant that Derek and I aren't really going out or anything yet. We've only had one date."

"But you'll go out with him again?"

"Possibly." *You'll have to pry me off of him with a crowbar.*

"Well, when it's clearly serious—say, after the third or fourth date—then we'll have that dinner."

I decided not to argue with her anymore. Derek's parents would never come to dinner at our house, anyway. The invitation itself might embarrass me, but it would never go any further than that. So I just nodded and said good night, and we went into our separate rooms.

Mine was dark except for the streetlight shining in through the curtains, but that was bright enough to get changed by. I crept quietly to the dresser, pulled out my pajamas, sat down on my bed to take off my shoes, and almost screamed—for the second time that night— when the table lamp suddenly went on.

"Doesn't anyone ever sleep around here?" I said.

"It's late." Juliana sounded wide awake. She must have been lying there waiting for me. She sat up and crossed her arms. "Very, very late."

"Is it?"

"Tell me everything, Elise."

"Jules," I said seriously, "I am so totally in love—"

She bounced delightedly on the bed.

"—with Derek's house. It's beautiful and huge— like you wouldn't believe. There's a cineplex-sized screening room and apparently an indoor swimming pool but I—"

"I hate you." She leaned forward. "Tell me everything," she said again. "For real this time."

So I did.

twenty-two

On Monday, Derek, Juliana, and Chase were already eating lunch together when I entered the courtyard with my lunch tray.

They were talking about college as I joined them. Big surprise—it was all the seniors could talk about lately.

Derek was saying, "—for Stanford, but I know I'm not going to get in."

"Hi," I said, squeezing in next to him. I didn't even try to keep my leg away from his as I settled in. Now my goal was to keep the whole length of my thigh pressed against his for the entire meal. He welcomed me with a gentle squeeze of my kneecap under the table.

Chase was rolling his eyes. "You'll get into Stanford, D. Your grades are good, you're captain of the lacrosse team, and your parents are . . . your parents."

Derek scowled. "Colleges don't care about that stuff."

"If they're choosing between Joe Blow's son and

Melinda Anton's son, they're going to choose Melinda Anton's son," Chase said, reasonably enough. "I don't get why that makes you so uncomfortable."

"Because if I do get in somewhere, I don't want people saying I don't deserve it."

"Then change your last name."

"Wouldn't change who my parents are."

"Yeah, but it might—" Chase interrupted himself. "Isn't that your sister?"

But Derek was already leaping to his feet and waving at a slight figure standing alone among the tables, looking around. "George!" he called out happily. She turned and spotted him and immediately ran toward us. He met her halfway and gave her a big hug.

So this was the famous Georgia Edwards. She was taller than I expected and pretty, with long straight dark hair cut in a heavy fringe over her forehead and large blue eyes like her mom's. She could easily have passed for twenty, but she ducked her head like a shy little kid when her brother led her over to our table and introduced her to me and Juliana.

"I thought I wouldn't see you until I got home," he said to her. He had his arm slung over her shoulders and was gazing down at her fondly. As tall as she was, he was still taller.

"I knew it was lunch time, so I figured I'd come say hi." Her voice was so soft, you had to strain to hear it.

"I'm on my way to meet Mom at the Ivy. Jackie drove me—she's waiting in the car."

"It's great to see you, George," Chase said. "How's the East Coast treating you?"

"It's good. But people are already wearing their winter parkas."

"We just moved here from Massachusetts," I said. "I miss the fall. Are the leaves changing?"

"Yes! There's this one tree in front of my dorm—I don't know what it is—" She faltered. "I should . . . but it has these big spreading branches and the leaves are, like, flaming red right now."

"I know which one you mean," I said. "We had one of those in our backyard and I loved it. But I never learned the name, either. Something long and Latin."

"Et-tu-Brute-ica?" Derek suggested. "Semper ubi sub ubi-cus?"

"You might want to reconsider ever being a botany major," I said to him. "Scratch ancient languages off the list while you're at it."

Georgia giggled. "We have to take Latin at—" She didn't get to finish because Chelsea was suddenly racing toward us, screaming in delight.

She threw her arms around Georgia. "Oh my God! Why didn't you tell me you were going to be here?"

Georgia allowed the embrace, but she looked uncomfortable and quickly detached herself from it. I got the sense that the girls' devoted friendship was a figment of Chelsea's Derek-loving imagination. Good. I didn't think Chelsea was much of a threat, but I didn't love the idea of her hanging around the Edwards's household anyway.

"I have missed you *so much*," Chelsea said to Georgia. "We have to get together and totally catch up. Call me this afternoon, okay?" She turned to the rest of us. "Meanwhile, you guys totally have to see this. It's hysterical. I call it 'Loser Love.'" She pointed to a tree at the far end of the courtyard.

We all looked. Webster Grant was bending down to catch something being said by the girl sitting and leaning back against the tree trunk: Campbell McGill. They were too far away for us to see their expressions, but her face was tilted up to his at an angle that suggested total adoration.

"He moves on fast, doesn't he?" Chelsea said, and I turned back in time to see her eyes flicker to Derek's face and then—pointedly—to mine. She didn't even notice that Georgia had turned pale and was clutching her brother's arm tightly, just went on smoothly, "Oh, sorry, Elise—am I breaking your heart? I know you have special feelings for Webster. Was he supposed to save himself for you? Too bad for you your father's not famous." Maybe she thought that was wounding me, but her arrow hit a different target, and poor Georgia looked stricken.

"Chelsea," Derek said.

"What?" She turned to him with a catlike smile still playing around her lips.

"Nothing. Just . . . be quiet, will you?"

Her eyebrows soared. "Oh, are we not allowed to say anything negative about Webster Grant now? Just because Elise likes him? But *you* don't like him—I know you don't."

"Hey, where's Gifford?" I asked, just to change the subject. "I didn't see her in English."

"Sick," Chelsea said dismissively. "Too bad—she would have laughed so hard at *that*." Another nod toward the couple under the tree.

Georgia whispered to her brother, "I should go."

"I'll walk you to your car!" Chelsea grabbed her arm. "It'll give us a chance to talk."

Georgia cast a desperate look at Derek.

"Thanks," he said coolly to Chelsea, "but I haven't seen my sister in months and I want a few more minutes alone with her." They moved off. He stopped, looked back. "You coming, Elise?"

It was the way he said it, I guess—the way his "alone with her" automatically included me—that made Chelsea pivot on her heel and stare at me, her mouth flopping open in dismay.

Juliana had told Chase all about Derek and me, of course (and maybe Derek had, too, come to think of it), but Chase wasn't the kind of guy to go running to his sister with the latest gossip.

So it wasn't until I jumped up to walk with the Edwards siblings that Chelsea suddenly realized there'd been a shift within our little group.

I ignored her horrified stare, dumped my tray in the trash, and moved into my place at Derek's other side.

On the way home from school in the minivan that afternoon, I told Layla I had seen Campbell and Webster together at lunch.

"She really likes him," Layla said. Then, to my surprise, she added contemptuously, "She's such an idiot."

"I thought you guys were friends."

"Not anymore. She's been such a jerk since the other night. She kept calling me a baby for asking you guys to come get me."

"You did the right thing."

"Do you know she doesn't even remember that she took off her shirt in front of him? She told me I was lying when I brought it up. She can't remember most of what happened, just that she was having fun and I ruined it by calling you guys. It's so annoying."

"She should be grateful to you," Juliana said.

"Things could have gotten seriously bad," I said. "Those two friends of Webster's were totally wasted. And he's—" I stopped myself. I didn't want to say anything about him that would make them start asking me questions about how I knew so much.

"Anyway," Layla said, "no one in our grade really likes Campbell. Since I stopped hanging with her, these other girls I like have been nicer to me and I've started eating lunch with them."

"Good," Jules said. "But don't be mean to Campbell, okay?" I shot her an amused look and she added sheepishly, "I don't like anyone to feel left out."

Layla said, "What's so weird is that I still don't think Webster really likes her."

"He likes that her father's famous," I said. "Some people are really into that."

Layla made a face. "That's stupid. Derek Edwards has way more famous parents than Campbell, but I don't like him because of that."

"There are better reasons to like him," I agreed.

"But I don't," Layla said. "He acts like he's so much better than everyone else. He's not very nice."

"Layla!" Juliana said, horrified. "Elise and Derek—"

"She doesn't have to like him," I said, cutting her off. "In fact, it's probably best for everyone if she doesn't."

* * *

After dinner that evening, my dad asked me to come into his office and do the crossword puzzle with him. But when I got there, instead of inviting me to perch on his desk chair with him like I usually did, he pointed to the empty armchair across the desk and said, "Sit down a second, Elise. I want to talk to you about something."

He had that tone in his voice—the one that made me feel like I was in trouble. I tried desperately to figure out what I'd done. The only thing I could think of was that I stayed out too late on Saturday, but he hadn't brought it up before.

I got up the courage to look him in the eyes and was relieved to see concern there, not anger. But I was still confused. "What is it?" I asked. "Is everything okay?"

He raised his hands and pressed his fingertips together, then peered at me over the pyramid they made. He spoke slowly, like he was choosing his words carefully. "There are few things more difficult than resisting the culture around you, Elise. No matter how solid a moral foundation parents may lay down, an individual's values can always be corrupted by popular influence. And an impressionable young girl is even more vulnerable to societal pressures than others." He paused and regarded me, waiting.

"I have no idea what you're talking about," I said.

He sighed and leaned back in his chair. "It's just . . ." He raised his shoulders and lowered them again, wearily.

"Your mother tells me you've entered into a relationship with Derek Edwards."

Was that what this was about? "That's sort of an overstatement," I said. "We've spent some time together—that's all."

"Good. I'm glad to hear it. It didn't make sense to me anyway."

"What do you mean?"

"You and Melinda Anton's son?" He raised his eyebrows. "You're far too intelligent to date a mediocre boy just because his parents are famous."

I struggled for a moment, tempted to just agree with him and escape from the conversation as soon as possible. But it would come up again. Because I *was* going out with Derek Edwards, and sooner or later Dad would have to know it and be okay with it. "He's not mediocre," I said in a low voice.

"Excuse me?"

I swallowed and raised my voice a little. "He's not mediocre. Derek. He's not mediocre at all. He's kind of . . . I really like him, Dad. He's just as smart as me—"

"As I," he said automatically.

"He's nicer than you'd think. Nicer than I realized at first." It was so frustrating: my father had the wrong idea of Derek Edwards, but it was the same idea I'd once had of him. "I know his parents are movie stars and all that, but that's not who *he* is. He's so close to his sister—you'd like that, the way he defends her and looks out for her. He's a little hard to get to know, so at first I thought maybe he was stuck-up, but he's not. Not at all." I wished I could tell him about Layla and how he had come to her rescue and Campbell's, too, but I knew I shouldn't. So I just said, "He's a good guy, Dad. Really."

He fixed me with a sharp gaze. "And if his father's name were Joe Smith? And his mother's Jane Doe?"

I raised my chin. "I would like him just as much— and would probably have liked him a lot sooner because I wouldn't have made some wrong assumptions about him based on who his parents are."

He considered that. He still seemed a little dubious. "Historically, Elise, you've always been my most rational child—"

"I still am, Dad."

"Just give me your word that you won't get sucked into this city's value system—that you'll hold on to your integrity."

"I promise."

"All right then. I'll trust you to be smart about this." He patted the arm of his chair. "Now come over here. Let's do that crossword puzzle." Once I was seated close to him, he rested his head briefly against mine. "No one's good enough for you," he murmured, almost too softly for me to hear.

Then he sat up and pulled the paper toward us.

twenty-three

Diana's reaction to the news I was going out with Derek Edwards was more upsetting than Dad's because she was so congratulatory. "Excellent, Elise," she said, when I told her on the phone later that weekend. "That's really cool. So you got over the fact that he's a jerk?"

"I was wrong about that. He's really not."

"Because he really isn't or because his mother's Melinda Anton?"

"Because he really isn't," I said tightly. "And anyway, you were the one who thought I should be friends with him because of who his mother is."

"Yeah, and you were the one who got all self-righteous about it."

"I didn't get all self-righteous." I took a deep breath. "He's nice, Diana—that's why I changed my mind."

"Right," she said, and I couldn't tell if she was being

sarcastic or not. "So when do I get to meet him?"

"Soon," I said. "So long as you promise not to talk business with him."

"I promise," she said. "But if you see Melinda, you have to tell her about Dad's catering and how good it is."

"I can't do that!"

"I know. I wish you could, though. He needs the work." Then she said, "But it's really cool you're dating him. It's really, really, amazingly cool." A beat. "Hey, guess what *my* boyfriend's father does—"

"What?"

"He's a dentist." She sighed comically. "Nothing cool about that at all."

"Free dental floss?" I suggested.

"Oh, yeah," she said. "That's way cool."

I laughed, but I hung up later wishing I hadn't previously told Diana I thought Derek was a jerk. It made me look like I'd changed my mind for the wrong reasons.

Both Dad's and Diana's reactions made me realize how impossible it was going to be to convince people I liked Derek for who he was and not for who his parents were.

I said something about that to Juliana, and she said soothingly, "Don't worry, Lee-Lee. I know you don't like Derek because his parents are movie stars."

"Thank you."

"You like him because he's so rich."

"Very funny. I could easily say the same thing about you and your boyfriend, you know."

"I love Chase because he's the nicest guy in the world," she said, more seriously.

"Yes, well, as much as I like Derek, I can't—" I stopped abruptly. "Wait a second—you just said that you love Chase!"

"I know." She hid her face in her hands. "It slipped out."

"Do you think you do?"

"I've never liked anyone this much before," she said, peeking out. "That's all I know."

"And that's all ye need know," I intoned.

"Derek?" I said on Friday night, as we walked from the cinema to his car after seeing a junky action movie that redeemed itself only by putting its protagonist in so much peril that I had a constant excuse to cling to Derek's arm.

"What?" Actually, I don't think he said the word, but his hand squeezed mine in an unmistakably questioning way.

"Did you start to like me because I was mean to you?"

He laughed. "Why? Do I seem like a masochist?"

"I know it's a weird question. But I started wondering why you liked me—I didn't see a lot of good reasons—and I thought maybe it was because so many of the other girls fawn all over you and you hate that. So maybe you liked that I was kind of mean to you."

He stopped and leaned against a tree trunk, thinking. Then he held his arms out and I moved into them. "It wasn't meanness," he said. "That's the wrong word. But I guess maybe on some level I liked that you were . . . challenging."

"Challenging?" I repeated. "That's what you call a little kid who's a pain in the butt."

"Fits you, doesn't it? Plus you were funny and cute and nice to your sister. I liked that you were willing to get wet for her. And I liked that when you were wet, you smelled like mint." He sniffed at my hair. "Still do a little, come to think of it."

"That's this cheap shampoo Mom buys. Juliana uses it, too, but don't start sniffing her. Or my mother. Or anyone except me."

"Mmm," he said, a little distracted now, nuzzling into the crook of my neck.

"Hey, look." I pulled away from him so I could point up at the sky. "A star. Seen by the naked eye. And Cantori said that wasn't possible in L.A."

He put his head back and squinted up at the darkness. "Actually, I think that's an airplane."

"Really? It looks like a star to me."

He shook his head. "It's definitely an airplane. That's

just the light on the tail—see? It's moving."

"Rats," I said.

"Disappointed?" He pulled me hard against him. "Did you want to make a wish? You still can, you know. Who says you can't wish on an airplane?"

I rested my head on his shoulder and closed my eyes. "Nah, I'm okay."

I had no problem wishing on an airplane.

I just couldn't think of anything left to wish for.